_____ Prologue _____

"YOU FORGOT to take the cash I left out for you."

At the low, unbearably sexy voice in her ear, Lani hugged the telephone closer. They weren't strangers, not by a long shot, but neither were they familiar enough with each other for her to joke about what the mere sound of his voice did to her insides. Shakily, she let out a breath. Her heart raced, and to combat the funny, weightless feeling that such a severe attraction caused, she leaned back in her squeaky office chair, lifted her tired, worn-out feet up to her desk and closed her eyes.

"Ms. Mills?"

"Yes, I'm here." He couldn't know she'd recognize his voice anywhere. She sighed and opened her eyes as she straightened. It wasn't right to fantasize about a client, no matter how much that client occupied her thoughts. Truth was, he probably occupied the thoughts of every woman in this small mountain town of Sierra Summit. Not that there wasn't plenty to do in the quaint, lovely place, but Colin West was such absolutely perfect fantasy material.

"Your money for your house-cleaning services," he repeated patiently. "You left it on the counter."

"I know. I'm sorry," she said, embarrassed. At the

time, she'd been flustered because he'd been watching her with a silent intensity that she didn't understand as she'd prepared to leave his house.

"No need to apologize, they're *your* earnings."

Again, that quiet yet steely tone. She was intelligent, she knew she couldn't love someone she didn't really know, but she could lust.

He was a man who knew what he wanted and how to get it, and if rumors were to be believed, he rarely ever let anything get in his way. "Ruthless and aggressive" was what they said about him, but Lani believed it was only a front.

To her, he wasn't frightening or even dangerous, but he *was* magnetic and passionate and fiercely private.

He also intimidated the hell out of her.

They'd known each other for one year. Lani had provided services for him once a week since they'd met, and though she had hoped their relationship would have risen above this stilted awkwardness by now, it was clear she was the only one who wished it so.

Sighing again, she shoved back all her secret yearnings and desires. "I'll pick it up when I come next week," she said. "Thank you."

"You're welcome." The husky timbre of his voice deepened, and for just a second, Lani thought that maybe it did so with equal yearning, but that was silly.

She was a nobody to him, less than a nobody.

THE BACHELOR'S BED
Jill Shalvis

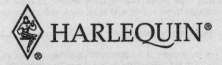

HARLEQUIN®

TORONTO • NEW YORK • LONDON
AMSTERDAM • PARIS • SYDNEY • HAMBURG
STOCKHOLM • ATHENS • TOKYO • MILAN • MADRID
PRAGUE • WARSAW • BUDAPEST • AUCKLAND

To Susan Sheppard, for always believing.

ISBN 0-373-25871-2

THE BACHELOR'S BED

Copyright © 2000 by Jill Shalvis.

This edition published by arrangement with Harlequin Books S.A.

Visit us at www.romance.net

Printed in U.S.A.

"I shouldn't have come to your bedroom," Colin said

"Then why did you?" Lani asked, sitting up. The comforter slid down to reveal more than Colin could handle.

His brow furrowed as he quickly raised his eyes to search her gaze. "You needed—"

"*You.* I needed you."

"You were having a nightmare. Anyone would have done—"

"Not anyone. *You.*"

Colin sucked in a harsh breath. In the pale light, his eyes darkened. "Lani..."

"Touch me."

She could hear his ragged breath, could feel his struggle for control. "It wasn't supposed to be like this," he murmured. "It was supposed to be uncomplicated. Easy."

"I know," she whispered, sinking her fingers into his thick, silky hair. "I know."

Even as he reached for her, he said, "This is going to make it harder."

"Well, I *hope* so," she whispered.

Dear Reader,

I would rather clean toilets than talk about myself, which leaves me in a bit of a quandary when it comes to writing you a satisfying reader letter. But since the heroine in *The Bachelor's Bed* cleans toilets for a living, it all sort of works out. While running her cleaning service, Lani dreams of things like marriage and commitment, but she hasn't found a way to make that happen. (I, on the other hand, found my Mr. Right and we have three wonderful little girls.)

When our hero (who never cleans toilets) asks Lani to be his fictional fiancée, she figures pretending is better than nothing, and—because he's smart and funny and has a job—she agrees. But we all know that true love is a sneaky emotion. It also conquers all, thankfully, which is what I love about romance.

I hope you enjoy how love works its magic in *The Bachelor's Bed*. Let me know what you think—you can write to me at P.O. Box 3945, Truckee, CA 96160.

Happy reading!

Jill Shalvis

Books by Jill Shalvis

HARLEQUIN TEMPTATION
742—WHO'S THE BOSS?

SILHOUETTE INTIMATE MOMENTS
887—HIDING OUT AT THE CIRCLE K
905—LONG-LOST MOM
941—THE RANCHER'S SURRENDER

What she made in a year, he considered less than pocket change. Her office was smaller and more cramped than the walk-in closet of his huge bedroom.

He probably didn't even remember her first name.

"Next week then, Lani," he said softly.

She hung up the phone, stared out the tiny office window at the Los Angeles Crest Mountains and smiled dreamily.

He *did* know her name.

"Next week," she whispered to herself.

THE FOLLOWING WEEK when Lani drove up to Colin's house, it looked dark. Disappointment filled her.

She'd rearranged her crazy schedule even though she could have had a rare day off, just to get a peek at him. It was all for naught.

She was an idiot. A lust-bitten idiot.

She walked into the kitchen and saw an envelope with her name on the counter. Inside was her money, for both this week and last.

"You won't forget this time."

Lani nearly leaped out of her skin at the unexpected, silky voice.

He stood in the doorway, filling it with his tall, dangerous-looking presence. She wasn't afraid of him. She didn't know why really, except that she knew all his dark beauty covered pain, not meanness. His gaze, as always, was inscrutable and measured, and every nerve inside Lani went shy. "I won't forget, thank you."

"You should charge more."

"I get by."

"You're worth far more." Colin said this sincerely, even as he remained against the doorway, cool and collected. Distant.

It didn't matter. She knew that was a defense, and she of all people understood defenses. But he'd noticed what a good job she'd done, and while it shouldn't mean so much, it did. Oh, it did. She smiled.

He stared at her, not returning the smile—she'd never seen him smile—his eyes for once readable. In them she saw confusion, which in turn confused *her* because he was always so sure of himself.

Apparently he didn't like the feeling, because he grabbed his keys, said a quick good-bye and vanished.

Lani watched him go, wondering at the flash of vulnerability she'd seen.

SHE DIDN'T SEE HIM again all month, though he always left money for her services. Twice he left her notes, complimenting her on her work.

She saved them and wondered how long it would be before he allowed them to run into one another again. Wondered also if he felt the connection between them, and if it unnerved him as much as it did her.

1

COLIN WOULDN'T HAVE SAID desperation was a personality trait of his, but he felt the cold fingers of it now. Frustrated, he stared at the calculated mess in his office. The building was deserted except for him. Even the downtown streets beyond the darkened windows were quiet on this late-summer evening.

His favorite time to work.

If he could, he'd work all night. Every night. Whatever it took to finish this project, he would do it, it was *that* important.

But he had to go home, had to ward off trouble.

It wasn't often he felt so helpless, and he hated that. There was only one thing to do—fight it.

Fight *them*.

The *them* in this case wasn't some terrorist threat or even a horrific viral infection, but something far worse.

It was his mother and her two meddling sisters.

The three of them had come together in their mutual campaign to ruin his life.

They wanted him married and they wanted him married yesterday, and to further this mission, they had sent woman after woman to him. They'd created parties, blind dates, "surprise" visitors, chance meetings, anything and everything to drive him insane.

He had no idea what the latest plan of attack was, but they'd been too quiet since the last one, when they'd sicced Ms. Mary Martin, the town librarian and closet nymphomaniac, on him. She had made his life a living hell for a month, smiling wickedly every time she ran into him, which had been disturbingly often. When she had goosed him in his office elevator one night, practically stripping him before he managed to separate himself from her, he had drawn the line.

No more interference by his family.

They had to be stopped.

LANI'S CAR barely made it, but that was little surprise. The poor clunker had been threatening to go all year and since she'd just recently put her cleaning business into the black for the first time, transportation had taken a low priority to other things, such as eating.

Carmen glanced at her with a raised eyebrow when the car lunged and jerked.

"Hey, it got us here," Lani told her worker as she shut it off. *Barely.*

Carmen read her lips, looking not so much grateful as doubtful. The woman was sixty years old and deaf. She also had a bit of an attitude and didn't do windows—not exactly perfect maid material.

But Lani was so short-staffed that she, too, was out

in the field cleaning today. Not that she minded since this was *his* house.

In fact, for a glimpse of *his* rugged, athletic body she'd clean every toilet in the house. With his dark, thick hair, even darker, fathomless eyes and full, sexy mouth, Colin West was truly the stuff secret fantasies were made of.

Sometimes she pretended that he noticed her for something other than the weekly maid. That he wondered how he could have employed her for a full year and not seen her mind-shattering beauty, her sharp wit. But in the end that was a cruel fantasy because he was perfect and she was...well...not.

Still she never stopped wishing, because someday she was going to take her great-aunt Jennie's advice—she was going to stop living life so carefully and purposely, she was going to jump up and take a risk and not worry about getting hurt.

Carmen sighed theatrically at the delay while Lani daydreamed. Lani knew she was going to have to stop hiring people just because she felt sorry or responsible for them. But it was a difficult habit to break. Besides, Carmen could be sweet.

The older woman stared at the huge house they were to clean and shook her head sharply, glaring at Lani. She huffed with indignation, which made Lani laugh. Okay, not *sweet* exactly. But she was company, which was nice.

It's going to be a scorcher of a day, Lani thought as she tugged and yanked at the heavy bucket in her trunk, panting a little under the weight of it. The mountain air was supposed to make a person strong, but Lani had lived here all her life and she was still on the puny side of petite.

Sierra Summit was located at the base of the Los Angeles Crest Mountains above the sprawling Los Angeles area, but still the July hot spell penetrated the altitude.

Lani swiped at her sticky forehead and hefted the bucket higher while Carmen watched, probably relieved she hadn't been asked to carry anything. The bucket was filled with sponges and cleaners and Lani wrinkled her nose when the strong aroma of pine and lime caught in her throat.

She had nothing against cleaning—it was her livelihood. But if Colin wasn't going to sweep her off her feet, which she had to admit was highly unlikely, then she might as well be back in her small but cozy office in town, working on her very-behind bookkeeping.

A sponge bounced from her bucket to the ground. Lani nearly killed herself in the juggling act she had to perform just to get it back in.

Carmen simply watched.

"Hey, don't worry, I've got it." Silence met this dry statement, and Lani found herself yearning for someone, *anyone*, to speak to.

The blast of unexpected self-pity was startling. She never allowed it, so why was she wallowing in loneliness today? "Because I just had my twenty-sixth birthday," she realized, speaking out loud.

Carmen watched her speak then snorted her opinion of that.

But, twenty years after losing the family that had been her entire life, Lani was just realizing something disturbing. Despite her inherent sunny disposition, despite her determination to live her life as though each day was precious, she had never again fully opened her heart to another. Guilt stabbed at her because she did have Great-Aunt Jennie, who'd taken in a traumatized six-year-old Lani instead of enjoying her retirement years. But still, Lani ached for something that continued to elude her.

Truth was, she wanted more from life. She wanted to follow Jennie's advice and take a chance, lower her guard. *Risk.* And if, in the process, she managed to have a hot, wildly passionate love affair with a man as dreamy as Colin, then so much the better, because she had to face facts—orgasms were but a blissful figment of her imagination.

Cleaning bucket in tow, Lani followed Carmen up the long, bricked walk of the upscale home, the early morning sun beaming down on her. She should be used to waking up on one side of the tracks and working on the other, but she still stopped to gawk at the incredibly beautiful home.

Her own place was a tiny modest apartment in an older part of town. Not seedy or even dangerous, just...cheap. She lived there for nearly nothing because Jennie owned the building and never let Lani pay what she charged everyone else.

But Colin's two-story, sprawling house took her breath away. The cedar siding had aged to the color of expensive whiskey. There were no less than three chimneys to conjure up the imagine of hot, crackling winter fires. Decking surrounded the bottom floor. Lani could close her eyes and imagine the swing she'd place where Colin would draw her down and whisper husky promises in her ear on warm summer nights. Then, beneath a sliver of a moon, he'd make good on those promises, using his hands, his tongue, his body until she was limp....

In the real world, she plowed into Carmen, who'd also stopped short to admire the house.

Icy liquid flowed down Lani's front, cooling her off.

Carmen frowned down at her own splattered tennis shoes and worked her lips in what Lani was certain was a colorful Spanish oath.

"Sorry," she muttered and, ignoring her wet shirt, kept moving, her gaze back on the fabulous house. She knew that Colin never used the fireplaces. He hadn't placed a swing on the deck either. His work was his life, and while Lani appreciated and understood his dedication, she wondered if he didn't sometimes yearn for more, the way she did.

As she came to the back door, she felt a strange thrill in her belly.

Would she see him? Would she catch a glimpse of

his deep mysterious eyes? Would she hear his low, mesmerizing voice, the one that turned her inside out?

She hoped so because he was the highlight of her week. He was incredible. Okay, maybe a little dark and moody, but positively magnificent. Maybe he'd be wearing those soft, faded jeans again, the ones that fit him like a glove, emphasizing...

Carmen tsked deep in her throat and Lani jumped guiltily, knowing her thoughts had been plastered across her face. "Oh, like you don't think it, too."

Carmen made the equivalent of a grumpy old woman's laugh and wagged her little finger at Lani. Then she wiggled her ample hips suggestively, pausing in her dance to shake her head. Lastly, she gestured to the cleaning supplies.

"Yes, yes, I know." Lani rolled her eyes. "We're here to clean. Clean, clean, clean. No hanky-panky. You know, it's amazing how well you can communicate when you want to. Maybe while you're in the mood, you can explain to me how you have the energy to make fun of me, but the minute we get inside you'll suddenly tire and let me do all the hard work."

Angelic now, Carmen smiled with a lift of one shoulder and a vague shake of her head. *No comprende.*

Right. Lani shook her head in disgust at the both of them. Every woman, young and old, within thirty miles sighed over the thought of Colin. He was rich, amazingly intelligent, gorgeous and, most importantly, he was single. That he kept his distance from people only fueled the constant rumors about his love life. It was said that he went through a different woman every day of the week—but that only made Lani all the more morbidly curious.

He invented *things*, for lack of a better term—electronic robotics. She knew nothing about that.

It didn't matter. She didn't need to understand to appreciate him. Colin worked hard, a good quality in anyone. He was driven and successful. His dark, dangerous fallen-angel looks didn't hurt, either.

Too bad he was so involved in his work. But unlike some of her other clients, who preferred to pretend that their maid was invisible, Colin West always nodded politely to her, spoke easily, and never made her feel less than the woman she was. They'd had many pleasant conversations over the months, and she could remember every one of them.

Enough, she told herself firmly. Ignoring the overwhelming heat, she headed quickly up the steep walk to the kitchen entrance, leaving Carmen huffing far behind.

Just as she reached the door, it whipped open, sending blessedly cool air into her damp face. Standing there before her in all his somber glory was Colin, looking unexpectedly wild, rumpled and just a little desperate.

"Thank God it's you."

"Instead of?" she asked in surprise.

"One of your non-English-speaking employees or, God forbid, the older woman who can't speak at all, the one who always sticks her tongue out at me."

"Well..." She thought of Carmen making her way up the walk right this very moment.

"Come in," he said a bit impatiently, his voice deep and rumbling. His dark, wavy, collar-length hair was more disheveled than usual and standing on end as if he'd been plowing his fingers through it. His eyes, so deep blue they looked black and fathomless, shimmered with what she might have suspected was nerves, if she didn't know better.

From what she'd seen, Colin West never suffered from nerves.

So why was his tall, well-built frame—which she couldn't help but notice was beautifully packed into a well-worn T-shirt and those snug old Levi's she loved—so taut with tension?

Lani opened her mouth to speak, but it fell shut again when his huge, warm hand closed over the heavy bucket she held. He set it aside as though it weighed no more than a penny.

His mouth was grim.

"What's the matter—" Lani squeaked in surprise when he pulled her the rest of the way into his kitchen, slammed the door and, with a gentle but inexorable force, pressed her back against it.

She should have spared a thankful thought for the deliciously cool house. She should have thought about Carmen, who was going to wonder why Lani hadn't waited for her, but her attitude-ridden helper was the last thing on her mind at the moment.

"Mr. West!" she gasped, even as she closed her eyes to fully enjoy the sensation of his incredibly hard body against hers. After all, if this was a dream, she didn't want to wake up. "Did I forget my money again?"

"No."

Lord, she felt good against him. *He* felt good. "So...this is to thank me for the job I did last time?"

"No." For a brief moment he pressed closer, and the almost-embrace spoke of a desperately needed comfort. She lifted her hands to his waist and squeezed reassuringly, trying to remember that he was a client.

"She's not going to let up," he said gruffly. "And I can't take it, not now, not in the middle of this project. It's too damn important."

Reluctantly, Lani opened her eyes because a *she* definitely ruined the fantasy. "Who won't let up?"

"It's enough to drive me insane." His voice was low, edgy and spine-tinglingly rough. "Only one way to stop her and—damn, you're wet!" His dark brows came together in a sharp line as he jerked back, staring down at his T-shirt, now clinging damply to his broad chest.

"I spilled. I'm...sorry."

"It doesn't matter," he said, still staring down at himself.

Lani stared too, because wow, with his wet shirt

pasted to that fabulous chest, the blood rushed right out of her head, which made thinking a tad dangerous to her health.

"It's the project that's so important."

She concentrated on his words with effort. "Project?"

"I'm designing a laser-surgery process," he said, pulling at his shirt. "It's so close."

"Laser surgery. They already have that."

"This is different—better." His voice told her how important this was to him. "Less cutting," he said earnestly. "Less time under anesthesia. It'll revolutionize the way surgeries are performed."

And would help countless numbers of people. Lani's save-the-world heart squeezed.

Her crush on him tripled.

"You'll save so many lives," she marveled. *A modern day hero*, she thought.

"The surgeons will save the lives." He moved close again, his eyes flashing with passion, and though she knew it wasn't directed at her, it made her dizzy anyway. Capturing her head in his big, warm hands, he tipped it up to stare down into her eyes. "But I can't finish, they won't leave me alone. No one will leave me alone. They want me out socializing, dating, spending the money I don't care about. I need help."

"You do?" With his long, powerfully built body against hers it was hard to imagine him needing help from someone like her.

"I need a fictional fiancée." His gaze held hers captive. "I know how this sounds, Lani, but will you marry me? For pretend?"

The situation finally overcame Lani's sensory pleasure. Yes, she was plastered up against the door, held there by the fabulous body she'd fantasized over for months, but had he just really asked... "M-m-marry you?" She hadn't stuttered since kindergarten, nearly twenty years before, but suddenly her tongue kept tripping over itself. "B-b-but..."

At that moment, Carmen finally made it to the back door and knocked with enough pressure to wake the dead.

Lani ignored her. "Did you really just ask me to...?"

"Yes." Colin drew a deep, ragged breath. "I've thought about it, planned it all out. I know this is a huge imposition, and I promise to compensate you...." At her soft sound of dismay, he hurried on. "I'm not trying to insult you, but I'm aware of what I'm asking and that it's an inconvenience, to say the least."

She couldn't help it, she laughed.

He frowned. "This isn't funny."

"No, it's not," she agreed. *An inconvenience to be married to him?* Not likely.

"It won't be easy, but I've watched you all year now. You're smart, funny and, best yet, even-tempered. We can do this."

He'd watched her all year.

At her expression, he hesitated. "You understand, this is *pretend*. I just need the *pretense* of being engaged while I finish my project." His hands were still on her face. Rough skin, tender touch. "Lani?"

Maybe she ought to vow to risk more often because, holy cow, this was more like the thrilling life she'd dreamed about for herself since she'd been a young girl remembering her happy, romantic parents. During those first painful years she'd wondered what kind of man would eventually sweep her off her feet. She'd wondered as time had gone by as well, even as she put up mental barriers to avoid the intimacy she so feared.

Now Colin wanted her.

No, she corrected, he *needed*, not wanted. There was a difference and she would do well to remember it. His proposed arrangement was too easy to romanticize. Colin needed time for his laser project, which would save countless thousands. She could be a part of that altruistic cause by helping him out.

And be married to him at the same time.

Carmen pressed her face against the window in the door, ruining the moment, glaring over Lani's shoulder as she tried to see. When she caught sight of Colin wrapped around Lani, her eyes widened comically.

Lani turned her head and concentrated on the warm male pressed against her.

"I just need your agreement," Colin urged in that rough yet silky voice.

It wasn't that she wasn't paying attention, she was. Yet she couldn't help but wonder—how did an inventor get such a great body? She'd seen plenty of great bodies before, but she so rarely had one held against her this way. It made thinking curiously difficult.

"I know this is really sudden, and a big decision, but I can't work like this." Colin dropped his forehead to hers. "I have to have more peace and quiet. It's crucial."

"I understand." His mouth was close enough to kiss if she just leaned forward a fraction of an inch. Her heart raced.

"It's urgent we resolve this before—" The phone rang, echoing strangely in his large house. "Damn."

It rang and rang, in tune now to Carmen's persistent and annoying knocking.

Colin's eyes seemed even more wild, more desperate, and because she'd never seen him anything less than completely put together, it startled her.

"Will you help me?" he asked.

"Well..."

"We're not strangers."

"Uh...no. But..."

"And you know I'm not a mass murderer," he urged. "Or a criminal of any kind."

"Yes. But..."

"Lani." He stepped close again, but didn't touch her. "I'll give you anything in my power, just name it. Money?"

"No!"

"A trip somewhere?"

Lani knew her eyes had lit up; she'd never had the chance to go anywhere. "I would never accept such a thing."

"Hawaii," he said rashly.

Hawaii. A personal fantasy of hers. "No. No, thank you," she added gruffly, knowing she was going to regret this in the deep dark of the night.

"I'll do *anything* for you in return," he assured her. "Your business...could you use another client?"

Only desperately. "Sure."

"Then please, add my downtown building to your client list. Daily."

Just like that, he'd upped her income. Not only upped it, probably tripled it. He could have no idea what that meant to her, and though she knew it was a pity that he felt he had to offer a bribe, she shamelessly took it, thinking of the extra hours she'd be able to offer her employees. "That's...very generous. Thank you."

"Will you do it?"

Despite her little fantasies, Lani was commitment shy, always had been. She was intelligent enough to realize that most of what made her life so good was the fact that she concentrated on others rather than on herself. The town of Sierra Summit was fairly small, only about seven thousand people in all, and she mothered, sistered and babied a good many of them. Her business was struggling constantly to break even, but only because she didn't charge enough and hired people who needed her more than she needed them. Her business handled mostly industrial work because there weren't too many residents who needed or could afford a housecleaner—Colin being the exception, of course. It wasn't much of an effort to keep everyone happy and satisfied, and Lani genuinely cared about them all, but even so, she still managed to hold everyone at a distance.

This came from a deeply ingrained fear of getting involved, of getting hurt. Whether it went back to losing her family so young or to something much more simple—her own basic shyness, for example—she didn't know and didn't often try to analyze. Colin had said this would be just for show, but she didn't fool herself, it would be complicated, and as a rule she didn't do complicated well.

Stalling, she offered a crooked smile as he once again pulled his wet shirt away from his body. "I don't really know you," she said finally.

The phone rang again and Colin cursed under his breath. His shoulders sagged and his eyes went even more wild.

Carmen knocked.

Colin growled and yanked the door open. In contrast to the tension pouring from him, he spoke slowly, distinctly, and appeared surprisingly calm, considering how white his knuckles were on the knob. "I need another moment with your boss," he said through his teeth, which were bared in a mockery of a smile. He waited until Carmen read his lips and nodded reluctantly. "*Alone,*" he added firmly when Carmen would have entered.

The older woman's eyebrows disappeared into her hairline, but she backed off the threshold. As she turned away, she stuck her tongue out at him.

Lani held her breath, but he didn't seem to notice.

Colin shut the door. His gaze whipped back to Lani, and there was no mistaking his recklessness now. "It's not all that difficult an issue," he assured her. "I'm an open book. Truly."

Lani let out a little laugh, for he was the most closed-mouthed person she'd ever known. And also, something else bothered her—why *her?* Surely he could have asked anyone and got a resounding *oh boy, pretty please, yes!*

Her silence must have scared him. "All right." He plowed his fingers through his hair as he turned in a slow circle. "You want to know me." He faced her and shrugged. "It's simple, really. I'm...technically inclined. I don't drink or do drugs...I like fast, sleek, sexy cars...and I'm fairly certain I don't snore."

When the phone rang yet again, his words came faster. "I like classical music, smart dogs and spicy Mexican food. And I always put the seat down. *Now,*" he added tightly over the annoying phone, "will you agree?"

Lani would never know what came over her, whether it was the unexpected flash of loneliness she'd experienced that morning, or just the deep, inexplicable yearning she felt for this man.

Risk, she reminded herself.

Help him with his great project. *Help him help you out of the rut your life has become.* "Okay," she whispered. Because that sounded weak, she licked her lips and simply, confidently said, "Yes."

Surprise flitted across his features and he held himself very still, clearly unsure if he'd heard correctly. "Did you just say yes?"

"Yes." Oh, God, she couldn't believe she was going to do this. "I mean, what the heck. I love spicy Mexican food, too. Let's do it."

2

THE TENSION DRAINED from Colin's shoulders and while he didn't quite smile, some of the strain left the lines around his mouth. "Well," he said, obviously relieved.

"Yes. Well." Lani grabbed her broom and laughed again, a little giddily. "I feel swept off my feet."

"For pretend," he clarified, eyes sharp on hers. "You feel swept off your feet for *pretend*."

Darn, she had a pesky habit of forgetting that. "Right."

He opened his mouth to say something, but Carmen stuck her face against the glass again, looking like a troll doll as she scrunched up her features to see better. Colin held up his finger for another minute.

Carmen rolled her eyes and disappeared.

"Um...Mr. West?"

He smiled at Lani for the first time, and wow, it was a stunner. "I think under the circumstances," he said, "you can call me Colin."

"Okay." Lani smiled back, feeling a little dazed. What had she done? Had she really agreed to marry this wild, untamed creature just because her life needed a boost? "I should clean now."

"Okay." He frowned, plucking again at his wet shirt. "Ouch."

"Yeah, the cleaner is starting to burn a bit," Lani admitted regretfully, shifting uncomfortably herself. "I'm sorry."

Without another word, Colin pulled the shirt over his head and tossed it aside.

Oh, man. *Oh, man.* He was perfect. Wide sinewy shoulders, hard chest, flat belly, lean hips, and the most amazing eyes that drew her right in... She was getting light-headed, and it most definitely wasn't from the cleaner fumes.

Colin ran a hand over his bare chest with obvious relief. "Better."

Better, Lani agreed silently. There was a solid thunk behind her. Carmen had banged her forehead on the glass attempting to get a better look.

The phone rang again and Colin sighed resolutely. "I have to get that." He looked as though he'd rather face a firing squad. "But I'll be back. We have to go over some things."

Lani nodded, wondering if some of those things involved her wifely duties.

Now why did just the thought of that give her a heady rush of anticipation? She wasn't promiscuous, not by a long shot, but somehow, with a man like

Colin, she thought she might learn something about being a woman.

Yep, the chemicals in the cleaning stuff she used were most definitely going to her head—and really starting to burn her skin. Too bad she couldn't rip her shirt off, too. At the thought, she let out another laugh.

"Lani?" Colin dipped his head down a little so he could see into her eyes. "Don't leave yet."

Did he honestly think she'd disappear now? He didn't know much about her if—

What was she thinking?

He knew *nothing* about her. Still speechless, a truly unusual state for her, she shook her head.

She wouldn't leave.

He looked at her for a long moment, and she wondered what was going through his mind, what he saw in her.

Again, the enormity of what she'd agreed to do staggered her. What was she going to tell Great-Aunt Jennie, who was likely to be so excited to have wed off her old-maid niece, finally? She'd have a heart attack!

It was just pretend, she reminded herself. No real heart involved. Walk away when the project's done.

Lani watched her half-naked boss—and, good Lord, her future husband—as he walked out of the room.

Another unstoppable giggle escaped and she

slapped her hand over her mouth. Giggling wouldn't do, it didn't become the future Mrs. West. "Oh, my God."

Quietly, and since her knees were very weak, quickly, with a wide, silly grin on her face, she sank to the nearest seat, which happened to be the floor.

THE PHONE had stopped ringing by the time Colin got to his home office, which suited him.

Everything was good, he thought with relief. He had his fictional fiancée, and now, finally, he could concentrate on his work.

All other troubles faded away as he did just that, with a hyper-focus born of necessity. Nothing intruded, not the Institute's hurry for his completed laser, not the fact he still had to talk to his well-meaning if meddling mother, nor that he had conned his cleaning lady into a pretense she clearly wasn't prepared for.

His fingers raced over the keyboard of his computer, his mind locked deep in the complicated equations he was formulating. He was so close to perfecting his compact mini-laser, all he needed was time, *uninterrupted* time.

Turning to the console behind his desk, he lifted part of the scale model of his invention. He worked on many projects at a time for various conglomerates and institutions all over the world, but he had also incorporated himself. Generally he worked out of a large converted warehouse downtown, but this home office allowed him the privacy he sometimes craved.

The laser component hummed when he activated it. A miracle, and the miracle lay in the palm of his hand. Finally, after months and months of work, everything had begun to gel. Just as he let out a rare smile in response to the thrill of that, the phone rang, startling him from his intense concentration.

Blowing out a breath of frustration, he grabbed the phone.

"Darling, you haven't returned a single one of my calls," said his mother before he had a chance to open his mouth.

Thirty-two years old and that tone could still plant a headache between his eyes as fast as lightning. "I know. I—"

"How are you? I hope you're good, you work too hard. Listen darling, I'm in town for the night only. I'm at the Towers with Aunt Bessie and Aunt Lola."

Oh, God, all three of them at once. They were just women; petite, innocuous, elderly. But together, this team of New York, Italian, Catholic-raised siblings had guilt-laying and conformity-forcing down to a science. Colin was convinced that together they could have conquered Rome in a day.

And now they were in town. He rubbed his temples, knowing they cared about him beyond reason, which made it all the more difficult to hurt them in any way. "I thought you were going to be traveling all summer."

"We are, we're just back to check on things."

Namely, *him*.

Since his mother had been the only sister to have a child, the three of them felt they co-owned him. Growing up, Colin had been raised by committee. His father had bowed out under pressure; after all, he was only one man. As a result, Colin had been fiercely watched over, fiercely disciplined and fiercely loved.

He was *still* fiercely loved, he had no doubt.

He just wished they would do it from a greater distance. Jupiter, maybe.

"I wanted to remind you," his mother said. "Muffy is expecting you tonight." She paused, then delivered the coup de grâce. "I've confirmed that you will attend."

"Now wait a minute...."

"We want to see you, darling. How long has it been?"

Only two months, he thought desperately. Had she and his aunts only been on their annual shopping trek in Europe for eight short weeks? He struggled for patience, in short supply on the best of days and this wasn't one of them. "We've spoken every week," he reminded her firmly but gently, not pointing out that even from a distance of thousands and thousands of miles, she still tried to run his life. "And I'm not going to the auction."

"*Charity* auction," she corrected him. "It's expected, Colin. It's why we came back into town. Everyone will be there."

Gritting his teeth to bite back his comment, he opened the delicate machinery in front of him and adjusted the micro-module with one of his tiny precision tools. "I can't. I have a—"

"Oh, Colin, I do so love you."

His heart softened. "I'm still not going."

"Please? Do this for me. Honey, I don't want to be a hundred years old before you make me a grandmother. I—"

"Stop!" He managed to interrupt and let out a short laugh. "Stop with the old. You and your sisters are the youngest old biddies I know."

"Oh, you." But his mother laughed, too. "This is the second time you've disappointed Muffy. Take a break from building those robot thingies and come out with us tonight." Her voice gentled. "Have a social life, darling. You need to get married again and do it right this time. Please? For me."

He might have laughed, if she were kidding. But she never kidded when it came to this—seeing her only child taken care of in what she saw as matters of the heart.

"Please don't hurt my feelings on this," she said in

that quietly devastated voice all mothers have per-
fected.

Guilt. *Dammit.* "You made the plans without con-
sulting me."

"Because you won't make plans for yourself! Your
divorce has been final for five years, Colin. *Five*
years. Move on. Please, darling. For me. Move on."

The pain that slashed through him had nothing to
do with his ex-wife. Lord, he needed a major pain
killer. A bottle of them. Instead, he lifted another
part of his advanced scale and ran a knowing finger
over the trouble spot—the laser shaft. Complex
plans for repair tumbled in his head.

"I'm simply trying to better your life."

He could think of several ways to do that, starting
with leaving him alone. Especially since with or
without this project he was currently obsessing over,
he would never again "better his life" with another
female. "Save yourself the trouble, Mother."

"But I want to die in peace."

He rolled his eyes. Great. Now the death speech,
when she was healthier than anyone he knew and
likely to outlive him by thirty years.

"Just one night," she urged. "That's all I'm asking.
Maybe she's the one..."

"No." He stretched his long, cramped legs over
the top of his cluttered desk. No one was the one. No
one ever would be again. "I've been trying to tell
you, I have a good reason for not wanting to date."

"Oh, no," she whispered, horrified. "I knew it! I knew it wasn't safe to let you play with dolls when you were younger!"

"Mother..."

She groaned theatrically. "Oh, no. *Oh, no!* How am I supposed to get grandkids now?"

He wisely contained his laughter. "No, Mother, that's not it. I'm...engaged."

The silence was deafening.

"Mother?"

"To whom?" she asked weakly.

"Her name is Lani Mills."

"What does she do?"

"She runs her own cleaning business."

"Oh." She thought this over. "Does she love you?"

Colin wasn't sure he knew the meaning of the word. Still, he remembered how wide- and wild-eyed his little cleaning lady had got when he'd removed his shirt. He hadn't thought he could be sensual standing in his own kitchen doused in cleaning fluid, but the way she'd looked at him had certainly put a spin on things. "She's...crazy about me," he said.

"Colin, are you sure? Really, really sure? I mean if she doesn't totally love you, then—"

"I thought you wanted me married," he teased. "Well now I have a fiancée, so no more dates! In fact, no more calls about dates. No more making *other* people call me about dates. Okay? Tell everyone."

"She's the one for you? You're sure? How do you know?"

Lani was quirky. Sweet and kind and exceptionally patient. After knowing her for one year, Colin knew she was a positive ray of sunshine that he usually tried to avoid at all costs, because to see someone so happy...it hurt in a way he didn't quite understand.

They were polar opposites and therefore, no, she was most definitely not the *one* for him. But he had to do this, had to be left alone to finish the project. His work was everything, it meant the difference between life and death to others.

It also meant a lie to someone he cared about, his mother. "I'm sure," he said quietly.

"But..."

She wasn't going to let this go and he knew this was because she blamed herself for his own last failure. He couldn't let her do that again. "I'm sure because—" he glanced out his window and saw Lani's small car parked there "—we're staying together," he improvised.

"You mean you're living together?"

"Yes," he said, sealing the lie with yet another, hating how he felt about the deception. "I have to go."

"Wait! I want to meet her. Your aunts will want to meet her, and, oh, damn, we've got a flight out in the morning. No problem," she said, quickly reversing herself. "We'll cancel. Your father can wait. We have to come stay with you, of course, for at least two weeks, that's how long we'll need to get to know Lani, and— Colin, *don't you dare hang up on me.*"

Two weeks, good Lord. "Gotta run, Mother. I'll let you know when Lani and I set a date."

"Colin! You hang up on me and I'll come right now, I swear."

The threat wasn't an idle one, he knew she'd do it. "Mother...Lani and I need time alone, to..." To what? How was this backfiring when he had it all planned out? "We need to get to know each other," he said quickly.

"Fine. I'll give you two days, I really can't just stand your father up, he'll pout. But I'll be back after New York." Excitement made her voice shrill. "I'm so thrilled—we have a wedding to plan! Can you imagine the fun? See you in a few days!"

Colin stared at the phone when it clicked in his ear.

Irene West was coming here. In two days. For two lifelong weeks.

Suddenly it hit him. His fictional fiancée had just become—he had to swallow hard to even complete the thought—a *real* fiancée.

The implications were mind-boggling. Lani would have to stay here, pretend to love him.

Sleep in his room.

He couldn't imagine she'd be willing, which

brought him to another thought. Why *had* she agreed
to this in the first place?

It wasn't as though they were friends, he hardly
knew her.

Oh, God, his mother was coming.

This hadn't just backfired, it had blown up in his
face.

COLIN CLICKED AWAY at his keyboard, pretending he
didn't have time to face the mess he'd created.

Which he didn't.

"Sorry to interrupt." Lani poked her head in the
door. She looked at him with those huge baby-blue
eyes, framed by a golden halo of hair precariously
perched on her head. "I'd like to get in here to vacuum and dust, if that's okay with you."

Colin found himself staring rudely, but he
couldn't seem to help it. It was as if he was seeing her
for the first time, though it'd only been an hour since
he'd asked for her help. She was lovely, startlingly
so. How could he not have noticed before?

She'd also saved his life.

What kind of a person was so willing to help?

He didn't know another soul who would have
done so. Uneasy with that thought, and irritated that
he'd needed her help in the first place, Colin stood
and walked around his desk to meet her. "You're not
interrupting. But there are some things we should go

over, if you don't mind." *Some* things? It was laughable.

How to ask her if she was willing to put the entire charade on yet another level and attempt to fool the nosiest, most meddling, well-meaning mother that had ever lived?

Lani's eyes widened slightly as he moved toward her and Colin slowed, realizing she probably considered him a certifiable nutcase.

He would just insist he pay her extra, over and above her cleaning fees, which had always been surprisingly low anyway. He'd yet to encounter a woman not susceptible to his money.

"You...didn't put on another shirt," she announced breathlessly.

He'd forgotten. He still smelled like pine, but then again, so did she. Her gaze was plastered to his chest. Her cheeks reddened, but she didn't stop in her curious perusal of his entire body.

He felt curious, too, though it wasn't as easy for him since she was fully dressed. A strand of her long hair hung in her still-flushed face. The baggy, shapeless, drab-colored clothes she always wore completely hid her figure, but judging from the lack of meat on her arms, she was a bit scrawny.

Definitely not his type, he thought wryly. Thank God. To have been attracted to her would have made this whole situation all the more impossible to deal with. "I have a bit of a problem," he said.

She blinked, stopped staring at his chest, and went still. "You don't need me anymore?"

"Ah...not exactly."

She shot him a smile then, and it was a stunner. At the impact, he lost every thought in his head and then had to reassess the whole not-being-attracted-to-her thing.

"We need to set a date?" she asked.

"Worse." He braced himself. "We need to live together."

"Before the wedding?"

"It won't get that far," he said fervently.

"No...wedding?"

Uh-oh. She sounded shocked...disappointed. "This is just for pretend," he said slowly. "Remember?"

She laughed and quickly turned away, hiding her face. "Of course. It's just that I thought...never mind. Excuse me...I've got...something to do."

"Lani?"

"I'm sorry. I've got to go." She ran out of the office.

3

COLIN STARED at the empty doorway of his office. What had just happened? No way had Lani misunderstood. He'd made it clear that this engagement wasn't real.

Hadn't he?

Running back through the conversations in his mind, he went still. Yes, he'd made it clear it was all for show, but had he let her think there would really be a wedding?

Swearing, Colin went after her, grabbing a shirt on his way, but he was a split second too late. Both Lani and Carmen were gone, speeding down the driveway in her noisy car. Colin grabbed his keys and raced out into the searing heat after them.

Having no idea where Lani lived, he broke several traffic laws trying to keep up with her. And when they crossed the train tracks, bringing them into an undesirable neighborhood, Colin hoped Lani was just dropping off Carmen. She was, but as he again followed Lani, he realized she also lived in this area.

He waited until she'd gone into a rundown fourplex, then followed her. He knocked softly on her front door, which was ajar, but she didn't answer so he let himself in. Her place was stiflingly hot. Colin didn't know how people lived in Southern California without air-conditioning, and he hated that Lani had to.

But once he was inside the apartment, he found it much lighter and roomier than he had expected. There wasn't much in the way of furniture, but the small living room was clean and appealing.

He found her in the tiny kitchenette and when he said her name softly, she jumped, a hand over her heart.

"You need to lock your door," he admonished. "For safety..."

"I'm safe here." She turned away and tossed a sponge into the sink. For a brief second, before she flipped on the water, her small, calloused hands gripped the counter tight. "Why did you follow me?"

"You left before we were through."

"I didn't see what else we had to discuss."

So hurt. Dammit. "Lani—"

"What a fool I am, huh? I mean I knew it was going to be for pretend, but I thought we were going to actually *do* it, for pretend. How dumb! It was ridiculous to think—" She let out a painful laugh.

God, he hated the helplessness that swam through him. "I'm sorry. I didn't mean to hurt you."

"You're so far out of my league, I should never

have—" She broke off and her shoulders sagged. Strands of wild, curly hair hid her expression, but he could picture it well enough. Devastated. Humiliated.

Leaning around her, he turned off the water, his mouth forming explanations and apologies. In the confinement of the tiny kitchen their bodies brushed against each other. His arms surrounded her, whether he intended them to or not. It couldn't be helped. The insides of his biceps grazed the sides of her breasts and, completely without logic, his body hardened.

Silence reigned.

Lani faced him at last, her hands behind her, gripping the counter tight. Now their bodies no longer touched, but a mere inch was the only thing keeping them from an embrace. If she so much as breathed, Colin knew Lani would feel his illogical response to her. The pine scent coming from the bib of her wet, baggy overalls was overpowering, but beneath that, he caught the scent of Lani, sweet and sexy.

"I always prefer to be alone when I'm making a fool out of myself," she said so quietly he had to dip his head close to hear her. "Maybe you could just go away and pretend today never happened?"

"You're not the fool, *I* am," he assured her grimly, tipping her face up so he could torture himself with her hurt eyes. "I *did* ask you to marry me, I just never intended to actually have to do it. It sounded so simple in my head," he said, bewildered. "I have no idea how it got so crazy."

"I see."

No, she didn't. She couldn't. "I told you how I wanted you to pretend to be my fiancée to placate my family and well-meaning acquaintances so they'd leave me alone to work."

"Yes."

It seemed so ridiculous now, and feeling a little embarrassed himself, he offered her a small, tight smile. "I told you also that they have a habit of matchmaking. If they thought I was taken, they'd have to stop. And then I could finish my project."

"Yes, I understand."

"You do?"

She smiled tentatively, which gave him pause. It was one thing to recruit a woman to lie for him, quite another to tease one. He dated only occasionally, and he consistently chose women who were looking for no more, no less than what he was willing to give.

Somehow, he couldn't picture this little waif of a housecleaner being interested in a quickie affair with him. She seemed more like the kind of woman who played for keeps.

And while he wanted everyone off his back, he absolutely did not want to be playing games with someone he could inadvertently hurt. *Had* inadvertently hurt. There could be no attraction between them, none at all.

"So you *do* still need a fictional fiancée?"

"Yes," he said.

She nodded slowly. "But no wedding date."

"God, no."

"I see." A light eyebrow raised. "You wouldn't want to get stuck with the hassles of a *real* relationship."

Not ever again, he thought with a shudder. "It's not necessary in this case. But..." he sighed, "I just found out my mother is coming in two days to meet my fiancée. She'll want to stay at my house and get to know the woman."

"Oh. So now you need a *live-in* fictional fiancée."

"Yeah."

"Well." Lani flashed him a hundred-watt smile, which quite frankly dazzled him blind and left him decidedly unsettled.

This was a business arrangement, he reminded himself. No reason for her smile to alter his pulse. Hormones had no place here.

"I understand now," she said.

"Will you do it?"

She looked at him, surprised, then reached out and squeezed his hands. "You can wipe that frown off your face, Colin. I don't go back on my word."

The easy forgiveness startled him. So did the physical contact. Not only because she was surprisingly warm, but because he wasn't used to being touched for absolutely no reason at all.

He came from a family of firm non-touchers.

His father had never touched him, unless of course he had been tearing the hide off Colin for taking apart an appliance or blowing up the garage with his biology experiments. His mother wasn't a toucher, either, she had been too busy running everyone's life or traveling.

As a result, Colin himself rarely touched anyone, certainly not for no reason at all. Which didn't explain why he'd done exactly that earlier when Lani had first arrived at his house.

Suddenly Lani danced away, frowning and shifting uncomfortably, plucking at her clothes. The air hissed out between her teeth and she looked pained.

"I've really got to get out of this shirt."

Before he could blink, she unhooked the two shoulder straps of her overalls and shoved the bib to her waist. She was still amply covered in that shapeless, huge T-shirt. Colin didn't blink. After all, he knew exactly how that cleaner felt against skin. It hurt like hell.

No problem that she appeared to be stripping down in front of him, in a kitchen so small he couldn't breathe without nearly touching her. He wasn't attracted to her, not in the least.

Besides they were going to be living together. He could handle this.

"Darn it," she murmured, still wiggling and rubbing her chest, bumping into him with every little shimmy. "Darn it all." And with that, she ripped the T-shirt over her head, revealing a tight, cropped tank top. She closed her eyes with a dreamy sigh. "Yeah, that's better. Whew! That stuff burns after a while."

Colin opened his mouth to speak, but nothing came out. Her elbows brushed his chest as she lowered her arms, her thighs bumped into his. Now his jeans were beginning to cut off circulation, belying his self-assurances that he didn't find her attractive.

How could he have known that beneath her awful, huge clothes, his cleaning lady/fictional fiancée had been hiding a body to die for?

"I think I burned my skin in a couple of spots." With her head bent, her silky hair slid over his arm as she stared down at herself.

Colin stared, too. She was slender yet wildly curved, and he wished she would pull her overalls back up.

She drew a deep breath and opened her eyes, smiling at him in relief. "You didn't tell me how much better that felt!"

Speech was impossible. Her overalls had dropped to just below her waist, so he had a front-row view of her smooth, very flat stomach, her slim but curved hips, the outline of her firm, high, unencumbered breasts.

Good Lord. No doubt in his mind, he *was* attracted to his cleaning lady.

To his fiancée.

She flashed that brain-cell-destroying smile again. "You okay?"

He wasn't sure. He couldn't think. He remembered a bawdy joke he'd been told, about how men had both a brain and a penis, but only enough blood to operate one at a time. He believed it now. "Uh-huh. I'm fine."

"So we're going to live together to prove we're a loving couple."

A loving couple. Damn, but that was terrifying. Unable to help himself, he looked at her again, and felt his body's surging response. She was one of the sexiest women he'd ever seen. And he was going to live with her. "We have to fool my mother, never an easy thing," he said a bit hoarsely. He cleared his throat. "She has eyes in the back of her head, and..." at her questioning look, he sighed again, loudly, "she thinks we've been living together already."

Her gaze widened briefly, then ran over his body once before she swallowed hard. "Well," she said.

"Yeah. *Well.*"

They stared at each other, awkwardly. Colin couldn't get past her easy forgiveness, her willingness to want to help him. Or her huge, expressive eyes.

"It's certainly not going to be a hardship to live at your house instead of here," she said finally. "You have air-conditioning."

That wasn't the hardship he was worried about.

This was pretend, this whole crazy scene, and it would be over as soon as he could finish his project. Lani would leave, and in spite of the fact that he was discovering an attraction, he wouldn't hurt her by letting her think there was more involved here.

"My work won't change," she said, almost as a question, touchingly uncertain.

"No, I don't want to disrupt your work. Lani...I have to know... Why are you doing this?"

She tilted her head, a small smile about her lips. "Your project," she said simply. "It's unselfish and hopeful and full of promise. I want you to finish it. If I can help, then it makes me feel useful and a part of it."

"Is that the only reason?"

A flicker of unease crossed her face, then disappeared. "Of course."

He didn't know what to make of her, she wasn't like any woman he'd ever met. And they were going to live together. Her razor in his shower. Her toothbrush on his sink. Her panties in with his whites. His head spun at that last thought.

He wondered if those panties were as revealing as the teeny, tiny, little top she wore now. And oh boy, sometime in the past minute or so, she'd gotten cold. Her nipples, rosy and mouthwateringly perfect, were pushing at the thin cotton, straining for freedom.

"So we're on?" she asked innocently.

He was a dead man, but they were on. "Yes."

She laughed, dove at him and flung her arms around his neck.

"What the—"

She squeezed him close, pressing against him all those warm curves in a spine-breaking hug. Before he could lift his arms to push her away—and he most definitely would have pushed her away no matter what his hormones were screaming—she stepped back.

"I have work to do," she said with a laugh. "I can't be hugging you all day long."

He had work, too. Didn't he? He opened his mouth to say so, but Lani shimmied past him to hold open the door, her body and smile rendering him deaf, blind and dumb.

How in the world had he fooled himself into thinking this was a good idea?

IT WAS A BALMY, sticky evening, the kind only mid-summer could bring.

Colin wolfed down a quick bowl of soup for dinner, preoccupied with some critical adjustments he needed to make on his project. Forgotten soup bowl at his elbow, he sat at his kitchen table, furiously scribbling notes. He'd used up nearly the entire tablet when he heard the car.

It was hard to miss as it backfired, sounding like the fourth of July.

Then Lani was at his back door with a duffel bag and a smile that lit up the hot Southern California night.

Something within him warmed to match it.

He opened the door and she moved in, invading his space with her cheerfulness, her bright eyes, that sexy scent of hers.

At least she wasn't wet anymore, or cold, thank God.

But then again, it was hard to tell in the shapeless summer dress she wore. She'd layered it over a loose T-shirt and high-top tennis shoes, and if he hadn't seen her incredible body earlier, he could never have imagined it.

Before he could move away, she gave him a quick hug, which so startled him he froze.

At his reaction, she froze, too, and pulled back. "So..." She bit her lip, looking a little unsure of herself. "You did want me to come back tonight, right?"

His mother wasn't coming for two days. But Lani was looking at him with those unbelievable eyes and he didn't know what to say. And was she always going to touch him for no reason?

If so, it was going to be a hell of a long engagement.

He had originally approached this whole fictional fiancée situation as he would anything—management by objectives. It wasn't something he looked forward to, but it had to be done. And how hard could it be? They'd already known each other a full year.

Except, she was unpredictable. She was also too...*happy*, a definite personality disorder in his book.

She tugged at his hand to get his attention, and just that small connection had a current of awareness shooting through him.

Oh, yeah, he was in big trouble in the hormone department.

"I thought we should practice," she said. "You know...being a loving couple?"

Never mind that he'd thought so, too, before; it was no longer a good idea.

When he didn't say anything, she ran her teeth over her full bottom lip. "I don't know about you," she said, "but it's not something that comes naturally to me." She blushed. "I mean—"

"I know what you mean." He had to let out a dry laugh. "It doesn't exactly come easy for me, either." If she only knew he'd been there, done that and bought the T-shirt. But if he was ever stupid enough to marry again, and if his wife had the body of his pretend fiancée, he thought he just might attempt to learn how to be loving.

"I'm not that great an actress," she admitted. "I think I'll need a couple of days."

A couple of days would kill him. He had no idea if

he could keep his hands to himself that long. "I don't think—"

"Oh, but I do." She smiled angelically. "We have to be convincing, Colin."

"Yes." His mother could detect trouble five hundred miles away.

"We should also put an announcement in the paper."

Wait. This was becoming far too...real. "Why?"

She looked at him with that kind smile, the one she seemed to reserve for when she was intent on getting her way. "You want people to stop bothering you. There's no way faster to do that than to put the engagement in print."

"But..." But what? She was right, she was *always* right, he was beginning to suspect. And why was she so sweetly disagreeing with him on everything? *Dammit.* "Okay. Fine. An ad is fine."

Lani dropped her gaze, looked around at the kitchen she'd seen a thousand times. Almost nervously, she glanced out into the hall and up the stairs.

She was wondering about the sleeping arrangements.

"Come on," he said with another heartfelt sigh. "I'll show you where the spare bedrooms are. You can pick one."

She looked relieved and disappointed at the same time.

He could understand.

LANI PICKED the bedroom at the far end of the hallway from Colin's. Not because she found him offensive, but because she didn't trust herself.

Her natural, easy affection seemed to terrify him. He'd nearly leaped out of his skin when she'd hugged him hello. Just a simple hug, an affectionate hug, but he'd hated it.

He'd made sure not to come within five feet of her since then. And when they'd climbed the stairs, he'd shown her the bedrooms as far from his as he could get.

She didn't know what she had expected—that he would have suggested his own bed? That wasn't his style.

Still, she couldn't help but wish, as she followed his tall, lean, oh-so-watchable frame, that in this one aspect, their engagement was real.

He dropped her duffel bag on the bed that would be hers. "Let me know if you need anything."

Did he mean it? She doubted it. He had that expression on his face, the one that assured her he'd rather be at the dentist having a tooth extracted. Without drugs.

Well he wasn't alone in that. She had so many reservations about this farce they were undertaking! She could tell herself she'd agreed to help because she believed in his project—and she did. But she knew the truth, that it was far more than that. And she was scared.

Colin West was driven and focused, and if she believed the rumors, he was cold and aloof as well.

But it wasn't true, she knew this with all her heart. No one with eyes so deep and heated could be cold. All year she'd been drawn to him on some deep, primal level and while she might not understand it, she couldn't ignore it. Any of a million things could have happened to make Colin the very private man he was, and she understood that better than most, because for all her bubbliness, she herself was incredibly private.

What she didn't get was the sudden need she had to please him, to be with him. To make him happy.

"I'll be fine," she said quietly, and decided to face the music with a brave smile. "So what are we going to do to get to know each other?"

Given the way his eyes flared, she'd gotten his attention. In response, her insides heated and they both stared at each other like idiots.

It drew a laugh out of her, because they were both so obviously thinking about only one thing. She reached out and stroked his arm. "This is silly, you know. We're adults."

He stared down at her hand on him. "Yeah, adults," he agreed, those intense eyes of his heavy and shuttered.

Her inner warmth spread, pooling in areas she hadn't felt heat in for some time. "Maybe we'd better sleep on it tonight," she suggested. "We'll think of something. Like Twenty Questions, or another game."

He blinked and looked as if he'd rather face a firing squad, which made her laugh. "This was *your* idea, you know," she teased.

His mouth quirked, though he didn't actually smile. "I'm trying to remember that."

From outside came a distant clap of thunder. Lani jerked, thrown by the harsh sound. "What's that?"

"A summer storm is moving in." He glanced out the window. "We'll get some rain I hope. And some relief from the heat."

Lani had an aversion to storms, one that went bone-deep. Goose bumps rose on her skin as the sky lit yet again. A twenty-year-old fear goaded her. In the guise of saying good-night, she wrapped her arms around Colin and hoped he'd hold her back.

He didn't.

"'Night," she whispered, gripping him tightly as a crack of thunder hit.

Letting go of him was difficult, for he'd felt warm and strong and wonderful, but she could feel how rigidly he held himself. Trying not to take it personally, she backed off and plopped down on her bed, just managing not to flinch when lightning flashed again. When the following thunder boomed and the windows rattled, she nearly jumped out of her skin.

She really hated storms.

Colin hadn't breathed, not once since she'd touched him.

She swallowed her silly fear. "Colin?"

"'Night," he muttered finally. And then he was gone.

4

THE STORM came and raged, and Lani tried to be strong.

She dreamed, long haunting visions of things best forgotten. Her mother, warm and loving, smiling as she placed Lani's hand on her rounded belly, letting her daughter feel the little sibling just waiting for his or her time. Her father, laughing with delight as he twirled her around and around on their lawn.

In her sleep, Lani sighed and smiled.

And then came the images of their sightless faces after the car accident that had killed them both, twenty years before in a wild, unexpected summer storm.

Thunder rattled the windows. Lightning bolted. Lani lurched up, a scream on her lips, but it died, replaced by a gasp of shock at the shadow that sank to her bed.

"What is it?" came a deep voice.

Colin. He'd come. He was rumpled from sleep, hair tousled, eyes heavy. Chest bare.

Offering comfort.

And she needed it just then, oh, how she needed it.

Before she could speak into the dark, chilled room, he lifted a hand and touched her face gently.

It came away wet from her tears.

"Lani?" he murmured, bracketing her hips with his strong, corded arms as he leaned over her, his face close to hers as he tried to see her expression. "You okay?"

In answer, she slipped her arms around that warm, hard body and tugged, needing him close, swallowing her last lingering sob as he resisted.

Staring down into her eyes, he shook his head slowly. "You were dreaming."

Thunder resounded again and unable to control her whimper, Lani squeezed her eyes shut and tried to disappear.

With a low, wordless sound of concern, Colin gave in and his wonderful arms gathered her close. "Just a storm," he said quietly, stroking her hair as she curled into the warmth of his embrace. His rough jaw scraped lightly over her cheek. "It can't hurt you. You're safe here."

She knew that, but her fear was irrational, as was her need for him.

The rain hit the roof with a drumming, driving force. Wind howled and shook the windows. The temperature had dropped, cooling the air. More thunder came, and lightning, too, but Lani, locked in the security of Colin's arms, sighed. His mere presence soothed, drove back any lingering part of the nightmare.

It was all in the past, gone, and it could no longer hurt her. Colin was here in the present, bending over her, whispering words meant to ease and soothe, and they did. But his husky, still sleepy voice also aroused and, despite the storm beating against her windows, Lani reacted to that. She needed him and yearned to feel needed in return. Without conscious effort, her hips rocked to his.

Colin went utterly still.

She should be mortified, at least sorry, but she wasn't. His heat seeped into her chilled body. He was dressed only in soft, flannel pajama bottoms, slung low on his hips. Their bodies were connected from chest to legs and it was such an erotically shattering position that Lani did it again, that little uncontrollable movement with her hips.

"Lani."

Just that, just her name, in a gruff, warning tone that wavered slightly with his own, very clear, need.

Her heart thundering, she pulled him closer, feeling that if he didn't kiss her, if he didn't put his hands on her and make love to her right then, she would die. "I want you, Colin," she whispered, lifting her face to his.

His arms tightened around her.

"Please want me back."

In the dark, he let out a groaning laugh as they

both felt the evidence of his own wanting. "This isn't how to assuage a bad dream," he said.

"We're engaged."

"For pretend."

"It feels real enough right now, doesn't it?" She tucked her face into his warm, wonderful smelling neck and licked his skin.

He shuddered and groaned, and again his arms convulsed around her. "I've never felt anything more real," he admitted.

A gust of wind battered the windows on the outside, while inside the tension came from the heat of their bodies. She winced at a flash of lightning.

"Lani—"

He was going to stop her, tell her why this wasn't a good idea and she didn't want him to. "We could start now," she suggested quickly. "You know, getting to know each other."

"What happened to the game of Twenty Questions you suggested earlier?"

"Okay—if you want a question, how's this?" She nuzzled his chest, seeking, then finding a small, hard nipple, which she kissed. "Do you like that?"

"Lani—"

Warm flesh, inflexible muscle—he felt so good, so indelibly male. His heart thundered beneath her cheek. Her insides clenched at the delightful contrasts of him and she lifted her hand, cupping his rough jaw, drawing a finger over his wide, sexy mouth. Her other hand touched his hip to urge him closer still.

"Lani, this can't be real between us, you know that."

"I don't know any such thing."

"Look, you're no longer frightened," he said a bit desperately. "I should—"

Her fingers slid over his lips softly, halting his words. "You make me feel safe. Comfortable."

He closed his eyes and she brushed her lips lightly, so lightly, over his. "Please," she whispered. "Don't go." She felt at home in a way she hadn't felt in so long. Too long. She held no illusions about the man poised for flight above her. He was caught, locked in a battle between regret and arousal, but to her, it felt right. She had to convince him. "Colin."

"I shouldn't have come in here," he said finally. "You're scared and vulnerable."

"Why *did* you come?"

His forehead furrowed as he searched her gaze. "You needed—"

"*You.* I needed you."

"You were having a dream, anyone would have done—"

"Not anyone. *You.*"

"I can't believe that."

This breathless, weightless, needy sensation was utterly new for her, but Colin wasn't in a place to believe that. She'd have to show him. Her nipples were hard, with excitement not cold, and she arched up until her chest just barely touched his.

Colin sucked in a harsh breath. In the pale light, his eyes darkened. "Lani."

"Touch me."

She could hear his ragged breath, could feel his struggle for control. Rain slapped against the windows as he lifted his head and looked deep into her eyes. His face held a mixture of need and confusion. "It wasn't supposed to be like this," he murmured. "It was supposed to be uncomplicated. Easy."

"I know," she murmured, sinking her fingers into his thick, silky hair. "I know."

"It's going to make it harder."

"Well, I *hope* so," she whispered.

His lips curved then, and he set his forehead to hers. "I'm the one complicating this, aren't I?"

"Yep." To prove it, she wriggled and squirmed until she was solidly beneath him. Slowly she drew up her legs and wrapped them around his hips.

At the unmistakable invitation, he groaned and dipped his head, touching his mouth to hers.

"Finally," she whispered on a soft breath, which he promptly claimed as his own.

Finally was right, was all Colin could think. He'd wanted a taste of her since she'd appeared at his door earlier this evening, though he would have continued to deny himself.

There would be complications, he knew, but as he

kissed the corners of her soft, giving mouth, then her lips, he knew whatever would happen could wait until this storm that raged both inside and out passed.

It wasn't going to pass quickly or quietly, that was certain, not with all the heat being generated between them. The soft covers plumped around them, cozy, enticing. The kiss deepened, hot and wet and unbearably arousing. Beneath him, Lani's sweet body writhed, and the heat devoured him.

Before Lani, he hadn't given enough thought or care to kissing, it had always seemed so intimate, and he'd shied away from anything remotely related to that.

He was beginning to see how wrong he'd been.

The only sounds in the room were the rustling bedcovers, the rain against the window. And then deepening silence as he slowly pulled back to gaze, shocked, into Lani's face.

The room went bright as day with a bolt of lightning, followed by a boom that rattled the entire house.

Lani jerked.

"It's okay. It's getting farther and farther away."

"I know." But she swallowed hard. "I'm not afraid anymore."

Those huge eyes of hers were full of secrets that he didn't know. He didn't want to know, or so he told himself.

She took his hand in hers and placed it over her racing heart. His long fingers skimmed over warm, giving flesh and curves, and he groaned. He liked the helplessly aroused sounds escaping her throat, the way she'd plastered her delectable body to his. He liked—

He liked *her*.

And no amount of distancing himself was going to change that.

"Colin—" She tried to wrap him closer.

He was losing himself in her, unable to remember why this shouldn't happen.

"Now," she whispered in a voice that told him exactly how much she needed him.

In response, he found himself raining open-mouthed kisses down her slim neck, over her collarbone, nudging her plain white T-shirt up as he went until he got to...ah, a ripe, warm curve, just begging for his touch.

She gasped. "More. Hurry."

"I'm exploring," he muttered around her heated, sweet flesh. "Don't rush me."

Her arms slipped from around his neck, down the taut muscles of his back. Unable to keep still, he undulated his hips, thrusting against the soft core of her, caught up in a rhythm as old as time.

And suddenly, he wanted to hurry every bit as much as she did.

Lani gave him everything, her lips, her tongue, her

passion. He'd expected an awkwardness, that first-time ineptitude. Bumping noses, grinding teeth, but with Lani, there was none of that, nothing except for a horrifying feeling that this was exactly as it was supposed to be.

He'd had women before, even women he knew less well than he knew Lani, but never had he felt as though he'd been given so much. It made him want to give in return, as her hunger fueled and fed his own. Both tenderness and savagery tore through him, equally mixed. He should have known it would be this way with her.

He kissed her again. His hands danced over her body. Her legs were bare. Beneath his fingers, her body quivered.

"Colin..."

His name had never sounded so sexy before. Her eyes drifted closed, but they flew open again, dazed and unseeing, when his hands cupped her breasts.

"Colin!"

He thought maybe he could get used to the way she cried out his name, all throaty and full of yearning. In fact, he wanted to hear it again, so he held back, just palming her warm curves.

Her fingers clenched and unclenched on his chest, her head tossed on the pillow and, when his thumbs rasped over her tight, puckered nipples, she again gasped his name.

He smiled in satisfaction. "Is that what you wanted, Lani?"

She made some unintelligible sound that turned him on even more. This was like a project, he thought with hazy delight, only better, much better. He wanted to take her slowly apart and watch her explode, then help put her back together again.

"Lani?" He pulled her T-shirt all the way off, exposing her to his gaze. She was perfect, beyond perfect. He bent over her, his mouth hovering as he let his fingers tease. "Does this feel good?"

She squirmed beneath the torment. "Yes!" she gasped, reaching for him. "More. Please, more."

"Like this?" He drew a taut, aching peak into his mouth, laving the very tip with his tongue, switching sides in tune to Lani's soft, seductive moan. "And this?" he wondered. "Are you sure—" his tongue swirled over her, then he sucked strongly "—this is what you wanted?"

Her hips were rocking against his and he knew she was nearly mindless. He didn't know what had come over him to tease her like this, he himself was dying, hot, and so unbelievably hard. It had been so long for him, and he'd thought all he wanted was to plunge into her and seek the oblivion that sex always provided. But he realized he wanted more. He wanted her to take that wild journey with him.

"Colin..."

His name again, in that breathless, sexy, hoarse, needy whisper. "I'm right here," he promised.

She reached up to pull him to her.

"No, no stay like that," he whispered. He didn't think he could take her touch, not yet, so he held her hands above her head for a moment until he knew she would keep them there. "Let me...Lani, let me..."

And he slid down, down her body, delivering hot kisses over every inch he passed until he was kneeling between her legs, gazing down at her gorgeous, straining body. In the pale glow of the night, her skin was creamy and lustrous. "You're...stunning," he whispered thickly, unbelievably close to the edge and she hadn't even touched him. He was going to lose it, just staring at her.

He jerked when her fingers brushed against the taut skin low on his belly, and he gripped her hand in his. "No," he whispered, knowing if she touched him again, it would be over in one second, maybe two. "Don't, Lani." He held her immobile, staring deep into her hungry eyes. "Don't move."

5

LANI LAY STILL with an effort, aware of how exposed she was, of the way Colin was looking at her while she lay spread and vulnerable. It was nothing less than thrilling—with his nostrils flaring, his chest rising and falling rapidly, all that power and passion within him barely leashed.

Heat suffused her, and it wasn't embarrassment, but need, sharp and unrelenting need.

His hands cupped her face, surprisingly gentle. "You're beautiful, Lani."

She'd never been told that before, much less even thought it, but Colin's soft, genuine voice made her believe it.

His fingers trailed slowly, ever so slowly, down her throat, around her breasts, lingering, then over her belly. He met her gaze as he drew her panties down past her thighs, her calves, then finally off, tossing them over his shoulder as he rose up, towering over her. He touched his mouth to her neck, sucking and nibbling. Then he kissed her, long and hard, drawing the need out, intensifying it.

"Colin...touch me."

He merely smiled against her skin and dragged his mouth down to a nipple, where he spent another long moment.

She was going to die. "More!"

Keeping his mouth to her breast, he trailed a hand up her trembling, restless legs. "Where?"

He wanted her to tell him? In words? She didn't know if she could. Yes, somehow she'd lost every ounce of inhibition she'd ever had, but to actually tell him what pleased her....

"Here?" he wondered, stroking behind her knee.

Her hips thrust upward impatiently and he let his fingers trace higher and higher, circling ever so close, but not quite close enough.

She nearly screamed. Her body arched, her eyes closed tightly and she reached for him, stroking him through his pants once, twice before he managed to stop her. "Not yet."

It was his turn to gasp when she ignored him and stroked again. "I'm ready!" she whispered impatiently. "I am!"

"Hmm. Maybe after this...if you're good." He scooped her hips in his hands and brought her to his mouth, where he introduced her to yet another sort of delicious torture.

His talented, greedy tongue dipped, slid, probed and languidly lapped, coaxing an earth-shattering climax out of her. When she floated back down to earth, the rain had lightened.

No more thunder or lightning.

Her fear of it was long gone.

And she was cuddled in Colin's arms, against his rock-solid chest. His face was buried in her hair.

She realized *he* was the one trembling, his big body taut as a bow. "You didn't—I mean, don't you want—" The words tumbled awkwardly to a stop. "Colin?"

He kissed her, pulling away when she would have deepened the connection, backing from her when she tried to tug him over her.

"We can't." He groaned when she wrapped her fingers around the huge, hot, throbbing part of him that assured her that he still wanted her, very much.

She didn't understand. "You changed your mind?"

"Not likely." He rose, regret lining his face. "I don't have any protection."

"*Oh.*"

"Yeah, *oh.*" Tension outlined his every muscle. "I think we're better off in our separate bedrooms."

Her body was still on fire. She needed him inside her. "How could you not have...*you* know?"

At her disbelief, he let out a little laugh, but it held no mirth. "I'm not really in the habit of needing any," he admitted.

"You...*really?*"

"You sound so amazed." He lifted a shoulder. "It's been a long time for me, Lani."

She had no idea why, but the thought was endearing and her heart warmed toward him even more. She watched as he untangled his limbs from hers. Without any sign of self-consciousness, he adjusted his pants up and over the biggest erection she'd ever imagined, and grimacing a little, he walked to the door.

She called his name softly.

He stilled, the long, sleek lines of his back glimmering in the dark. After a second, he glanced over his shoulder at her. His eyes were still smoldering, ensuring her it would be a long, sleepless night for him, too.

She smiled, feeling almost shy, which was ridiculous after what they'd just shared. "It's been a long time for me, too," she whispered.

He smiled and it stopped her heart.

Then he was gone.

IT MIGHT NEVER have happened—the nightmare, Colin's magic touch, any of it, except that her body tingled knowingly at just the sight of him.

Lani pressed her hands to the butterflies dancing in her belly and, pretending she really belonged there, she let the swinging kitchen doors shut behind her as she walked in.

Colin sat at the table, expression intense, head bent over a cup of steaming coffee and a newspaper. His dark hair was wet and pushed off his forehead as if he had no time for such things as picking up a comb. The black shirt he wore looked soft and incredibly masculine, especially given that he hadn't yet finished buttoning it up. His skin was smooth and sleek and rippled with strength.

Her fingers itched to touch.

His long legs were stretched out in front of him, covered in slate-gray trousers, tailor-made to show off every exceptional inch of him. His feet were bare.

"Colin." The name floated off her lips in a tone of longing before she could stop herself, and he lifted his gaze, holding her hostage with nothing more than his eyes. He nodded at her, managing to hold all his thoughts safe and sound, giving nothing of himself away, and again, Lani had to remind herself that last night had *not* been a dream, but a hot, welcome reality.

He *had* touched her. He *had* shown her an unrestrained passionate side of him that until now she'd only fantasized about.

There was no further sound, nothing except for the little squeak Lani could have sworn her heart made at the cool, distancing look in his eyes.

Pushing his coffee away, he rose. He towered over her, all elegant, male grace as he moved to the door, clearly unwilling to spend even a moment with her.

He was probably afraid she'd beg him to touch her again, she thought, blushing, because she held no illusions, she *had* begged him last night. Still, she pushed her chin in the air, not having to force the spurt of fierce pride. "You forgot to take your cup to the sink."

He stopped, his hand on the door, and looked at her, clearly surprised. "What?"

Ah, he *could* speak in the morning. Granted it was a rough and gruff sort of voice, assuring her he'd not been long out of bed, which only increased the fluttering low in her stomach because he sounded so irrationally sexy. "I'm not your maid today," she reminded him. "Only once a week, remember?"

His eyes darkened and she knew he was remembering last night, too. She certainly hadn't been the maid then, had she?

"You're right. Excuse me," he said and went back to the table. He grabbed his cup and took it to the sink, though he didn't rinse it or put it in the dishwasher, just set it in the sink. When he turned and caught her eye, he lifted a brow as if in a dare.

She said nothing. She knew he rarely took care of his dishes in the morning because whenever she came to clean, there was always a stack in the sink. If he thought he was going to get a nagging pretend fiancée, he was in for a surprise.

Instead she called out cheerfully as she opened the door. "Have a good day!"

He hesitated, body stone still, and she couldn't resist adding, "Nice talking to you, Colin. You're so sweet and chipper in the morning."

He turned and faced her. "I'm never sweet and chipper."

"I hadn't noticed." She bit her lip. "We're not going to talk about it, are we?"

His eyes went wary. "Do we have to?"

"It might help."

"I doubt it."

"We're supposed to be getting to know each other. Glaring at me over your morning coffee as if you can't remember why I'm here isn't going to solve your problem."

He drew in a deep, ragged breath and let it out slowly. He ran his fingers through his drying hair. The scent of him drifted to her, woodsy soap and a hint of clean, healthy male. "I remember why you're here," he said.

How could he forget, Colin wondered, when he was still feeling her skin beneath his fingertips, still tasting her on his lips?

After he'd left her, he hadn't slept a wink. It had been impossible with his body aching and needy, his mind unable to forget the image of Lani in sheer bliss.

"Colin."

He nearly leaped out of his skin when she came close and set her hand on his. The top of her head barely met his chin. Her eyes were compassionate and full of things that made it hard to look at her, but he couldn't tear his gaze away.

"Don't, Lani. Don't say it. This is my doing, I know it."

She shook her head, her eyes warm and soft. And dammit, she continued to touch him in that comforting yet madly arousing way. It wasn't difficult to imagine how it would be between them if he said the hell with his decision not to mislead her or hurt her, if he pulled her body to his and slowly stripped off those ridiculously ugly overalls until she wore nothing but a hot, needy look on her face and his name on her lips.

"It'll work out," she assured him with a little pat. "You'll see." Her fingers ran up his arm and then to his chest.

He captured her wandering hand, but not before the sizzling connection aroused him. He'd slept that way, and after touching her, after watching her come in his arms, he just might sleep in that uncomfortable state for the rest of his life.

Her sweet, beguiling smile never wavered. "I'll put the ad in the paper announcing our engagement today."

How the hell had he done this to himself? he wondered, looking down into her eager-to-please eyes. "Lani, I don't think—"

"Now, I have to get to work, but don't worry so much," she soothed, gently pushing him out of the kitchen, dismissing him with an ease that was startling. "Being so stressed will give you wrinkles."

Wrinkles. He was about to blow the zipper off his pants and she was worried about wrinkles.

"If you'd like, after work I'll cook dinner. We should sit around and talk."

"Talk."

"Yes." She seemed amused. "We have to get to know each other, remember? Your mother is coming tomorrow. And I'm not trying to criticize you here, but you really don't have the look of a man madly in love. We'll have to work on that."

He closed his eyes.

"It's fine," she insisted, again touching him, slipping her hands around his waist. "Everything is going to be fine."

He remembered those hands, remembered how they'd encircled him, driven him to the very edge with those slow, sure, mind-blowing strokes—

His own groan vented the air.

"Colin—" She hesitated and he opened his eyes, looking over his shoulder to meet her unsure gaze. "Thanks for being there for me last night. You know, after my nightmare."

He'd worried about that, too. What haunted her? He hadn't wanted to spend any more time than absolutely necessary thinking about her, but nothing had gone as planned so far—he shouldn't have been surprised by the depth of his concern. "Do you have them often?"

"Dreams? Yeah. My favorite is the one where I get to go to Hawaii and snorkel."

"The nightmares, Lani."

She bowed her head, studied her fingernails which were short and unpainted. "Not too much anymore."

"What are they from?"

Her head tipped up at that, and amusement crossed her face. "What's this? Genuine curiosity? Hmm, maybe you're going to be better at this than I thought." Her smile faded. "Are we going to share a bed when your family comes?"

She looked suddenly unsure, vulnerable. He wouldn't hurt or lead this woman on, not for anything, not even to save his sorry hide. "That wasn't part of the original deal, was it?"

"No," she whispered.

"I don't want to make you uncomfortable. Ever."

"You won't," she said quickly. "And we really *should* share a bed— I mean bedroom. For your mom's sake."

He cleared his throat around the knot of desire there. "Yeah."

"Are you...um..." A red flush worked its way up her face. "You know, going to the store to get...what you need?"

It took him only a second to realize what his sweet little fiancée wanted to know. "It's not a good idea."

"I see." She backed away from him, her smile wavering. "Well. Have a great day, Colin. See you tonight."

Tonight. God, tonight. How could he continue to resist her? Having a condom would be little protection against the true danger—her worming her way into his heart.

After she was gone, Colin stared at the swinging door, the image of her expressive eyes imprinted on his mind. They'd held honest affection when she'd looked at him. Warm compassion. Humor. And hope.

It was that last emotion that was going to be the hardest of all to resist.

GREAT-AUNT Jennie tossed back some of her sparkling cider, heavily liberated with her not-so-secret stash of whiskey, wheezing when it went down the wrong way.

Lani shook her head with a shudder when her aunt offered her the jug. "No thanks."

"Let me get this straight." Aunt Jennie took another swig and gasped, pounding her chest. Her curls, the silver burnished ones she'd been paying Verna at the Body Wave Salon weekly for for the past forty years, bounced as she set down her drink. "You're finally engaged."

"Yes," Lani said. "But—"

"Engaged to the most eligible bachelor in town."

Great-Aunt Jennie grinned and slapped her knee. "Imagine that!"

"But—"

"Hold it right there." Jennie, who was eighty-two but didn't look a day older than sixty-five, held up a hand. She knew her niece well. "Honey, why is it with you there's always a *but*?"

Lani let out a reluctant grin. "And this *but* is a biggy."

Jennie sighed. "You're going to ruin this for me, aren't you?"

"It's likely," Lani admitted. Her great-aunt had not been the most conventional of guardians. She'd held séances, had traveled extensively, whipping Lani out of school on a whim, and had never followed any of the rules. She hadn't joined the PTA, had never made easy friends with the other parents or driven in the carpool.

But she'd been there for Lani when she'd had no one else, and for that she was grateful. Lani might have grown up differently than most, but Jennie had done the best she could and Lani would never forget it.

But she was well aware that her aunt's greatest wish was to see Lani taken care of. Jennie took it personally that Lani had a deep-rooted fear of emotional attachments. She wanted Lani to go the route of the very normal and expected marriage, no matter how abnormal Lani's upbringing had been. She wanted

Lani's future secure, and she wanted that because she loved Lani with all her slightly off-kilter, wacky heart.

Realizing that brought both a lump to Lani's throat and a shoulder-load of shame about the façade. She had to tell Jennie the truth about the engagement, had to make her understand that marriage, a true marriage, was just not in the cards.

At that thought, Lani's heart sent up a little protest, but now was not the time for self-reflection. "The truth is, it's just pretend, Aunt Jennie. Colin needs me to *pretend* to marry him, that's all."

"Pretend."

"That's right."

They were in Jennie's house, just a few blocks from Lani's apartment. It was run down on the outside, but the inside was a treasure trove, decorated with things from all over the world that Jennie had collected on her various travels.

There was not a speckle of dust, Jennie wouldn't allow it. Not on her things. She was Lani's toughest, hardest-to-please client, and also her favorite.

To get her thoughts together, Lani moved around the room, touching those things now, unable to sit still.

Jennie had gone quiet, but now she had a question. "What exactly do you mean, *pretend*?"

"Colin needs to finish a very important project

he's working on, but he's being hounded. He thought a fiancée would help."

"What's the matter with him that he can't get a real fiancée? Is he ugly?"

Lani thought of Colin's piercing eyes, of the lean rugged body that had left her breathless. "No," she managed to say. "Definitely not ugly."

"Is he mean?"

No one could hold her the way Colin had last night and be mean. "No."

"Uh-huh." Jenny's brilliant green eyes sparkled. "I get it. You just want to live in sin without people bothering you. That's okay, honey, I understand a healthy sexual drive. I lived through the sixties, remember?"

"It's not like that—"

"Hormones aren't easy to deny," Jennie went on blissfully. "Why in my day, we didn't even try. We just married young so it was all legal."

"It has nothing to do with hormones," Lani said weakly, grabbing for the jug of cider when the older woman reached for it. "You've been reading too many of those romances, Aunt Jennie."

"They give a woman a better sex life." At Lani's startled laugh, Jennie smiled and nodded. "I read that somewhere."

"Can we get back to my engagement?"

"Sure. What you're trying to tell me is that you're not really marrying him." Aunt Jennie studied a box of open cigars on the low table in front of her couch before choosing one. She didn't dare light it, not with Lani within reach, so she just clamped her teeth around it.

"What do you think of the whole thing?" Lani asked.

"Well, I think it's a damn shame, honey. Make him earn it. Don't give it to him for free."

"He has nothing to earn," Lani insisted, blushing in spite of herself.

"Of course he does. I hope he's going to at least cook, or do the grocery shopping."

"No, you don't understand. It's for show. All of it."

Jennie's jaw went slack and the cigar tumbled out into her lap, making Lani thankful Jennie's doctor had given her strict orders not to light up. She was a danger to society.

"*All* for show?" she repeated in disbelief.

"Well...yes." Mostly.

"You mean you're not...?"

"No."

Her great-aunt sadly shook her head. "Oh, honey. I taught you better than that."

LANI DIDN'T KNOW what she expected that night. Certainly that she and Colin would spend a considerable amount of time talking, gathering facts and coming up with a common story.

Colin was a planner, she knew that much. She knew how important it would be to him to have this all analyzed and prepared for his mother and aunts.

But she was alone, pacing Colin's large, eerily empty house. The house itself was beautiful; old, airy and full of character. The inside should have been a delight. But though Colin had been there a number of years, he had hardly furnished it. Most of the glorious rooms remained practically empty.

Lani wondered why. Her sneakers squeaked on the wood floor of the wide hallway as she paced.

She knew so little about him.

Why was he so private? What secrets did his dark, mysterious eyes hold? Did he ever share himself? What made him so leery of physical affection?

He might like to think that his cool, aloof front would keep people at bay, but not Lani. Oh, no. It only made her all the more curious.

Lani thought of last night and smiled. He certainly wasn't leery of passion, he'd been hot, earthy and completely uninhibited. That he'd made her feel those things, too, shouldn't have surprised her, but it did. She'd never felt so out of control in her life.

She had liked it very much.

So where was he?

She glanced at the clock for the tenth time in as many minutes. It was nearly 9:00 p.m. and it was becoming more and more clear that her reluctant fiancé wasn't coming home.

It wouldn't do to get annoyed. All she'd accomplish would be to raise her blood pressure because she did understand Colin. He didn't want to be tied to her, didn't want the commitment.

Neither did she, Lani reminded herself.

But Colin had been backed into a corner. He had no choice and, whether he realized it or not, he was rebelling. Pushing him now would be a big mistake.

Besides, his nonappearance could be an innocent mistake. She couldn't imagine Colin would ever hurt her on purpose, but she could imagine him in his downtown office, working frantically, completely into what he was doing, oblivious of the passing time.

Without stopping to consider the wisdom of interrupting the lion in his den, Lani grabbed her keys and was out the door. Typical of a Southern California summer, the night temperature hadn't dropped to a comfortable level, despite the recent storm. It was over eighty degrees and unbearably muggy.

It didn't stop her. Truth was, nothing could. She was driven to help Colin, and she wouldn't give up.

The building Colin owned and worked in was one she'd admired often. It had once been an old warehouse, but Colin had remodeled it to suit his own needs. It was made of an intriguing mix of brick and glass, and exuded character and charm, proof that Colin possessed both.

The reception area was deliciously cool. So much

so that Lani stood there a long moment, absorbing the breathable air. Then she followed a dim light that shone from down one of the two hallways. She came upon an office where a young woman was hunched over a set of books. Wearing faded denim, no makeup and a scowl, the woman was obviously not happy about her hours or her work.

"Hello," Lani said softly, not wanting to startle her.

Too late. The woman let out a squeak of surprise.

"I'm sorry," Lani exclaimed as the woman put a hand to her chest and took a deep breath. "I didn't mean to scare you, I'm just looking for Colin."

"Who are you?"

"Lani Mills, his—" *cleaning lady* came to the tip of her tongue, but she was much more. Wasn't she? "I'm his fiancée."

The woman blinked. "Colin *West?*"

The disbelief was understandable. Not only was Colin the most eligible bachelor around, he wasn't exactly known for having long-lasting relationships, much less an engagement. "Yes. I think he's working—"

"He's *always* working." The woman still looked stunned and Lani couldn't blame her, she herself was still reeling over the strange, unexpected turn of events.

"Yes, well...he's incredibly dedicated." Lani smiled. "I admire that."

The woman sighed and stood, shoving her huge glasses higher on her nose. "*Engaged*. Hard to believe. Well, I'm Claudia, his overworked, underpaid, not-quite-appreciated secretary." She stuck out her hand. "Maybe women will stop calling him now?" she asked hopefully.

"Women will definitely stop calling him now," Lani answered firmly. "You're working pretty late yourself."

"Special project and I'm behind on the books." Claudia stretched her back and yawned. "But I'm outta here. He's all yours." Her look said she wasn't sure why Lani would want him.

Lani should have left well enough alone. She knew better than to interfere, really she did, but she couldn't seem to help herself. She had a streak of loyalty a mile wide, it was deeply ingrained. She protected those she cared about, and she cared about Colin. "Colin is just very involved with his work, it's important to him."

"I hadn't noticed."

Claudia's soft sarcasm only made Lani all the more determined. "He's a wonderful man. He deserves employees who think so, too."

Claudia had the good grace to blush. "I'm sorry. I do respect him, greatly. He pays fairly well and the work is steady. I even get benefits. It's just unnerving to work for someone who can render any female stupid with just a look and remain so unaware of it, you know?"

Lani was afraid she did.

"He's so...well...distant. Remote." Claudia hesitated. "Look, we're both women. I feel compelled to ask you. Do you have any clue what you're getting yourself into?"

6

AT CLAUDIA'S WORDS, Colin came to an abrupt halt outside the office door. He'd been walking down the hallway toward the coffee machine. But now he stood rock still, waiting with a strange breathlessness for Lani to come to her senses and run like hell.

"Yes, I think I have a good idea what I'm getting into," Lani said quietly, her voice sure and strong.

Colin drew a deep breath and leaned against the wall. The emotion pounding through him didn't bear thinking about.

What would he do if she reneged?

Claudia let out a little laugh. "Well if I were you," she said. "I'd think twice about marrying a man too gorgeous and rich for his own good."

"Those aren't sins, you know." Lani sounded amused.

Still unseen, Colin cursed himself for not giving the still-pouting Claudia the new computer she'd asked for. Clearly, she wasn't going to forgive him easily.

"No, not sins," Claudia said, agreeing with Lani. "But he's not exactly an easy man to be with. He can be selfish as hell, and from what I understand, he's not very good at the marriage thing."

Colin went very still. It was all too true, so it seemed silly to be insulted.

He fully expected Lani to back out of their bargain, and found himself tense and straining, waiting for the damning words.

The silence was deafening.

What was taking her so long? Any second now, she'd let him down.

Nothing new.

It happened a lot, he reminded himself. Plenty of people needed him, counted on him, but in return there wasn't anyone *he* needed, no one *he* could count on.

Lani was going to disappoint him, and strangely enough, it was going to hurt. He'd thought himself immune to that kind of pain long ago, but apparently he'd been wrong because his insides were twisting.

"Oh, I know *exactly* what I'm getting."

At Lani's soft but certain voice, some of Colin's warmth returned.

"And he's exactly what I want," she went on. "He's not what you've described. Not at all. He's a wonderful man. Maybe a little wary, but can you blame him? He's hounded night and day by people wanting something from him. It'd make anyone uncomfortable."

"Look, I'm not trying to talk you out of it, I just want to make sure you know what you're doing."

"I know what I'm doing. His aloofness doesn't scare me. Not when beneath that is a warm, passionate, beautiful man. And I feel lucky to be marrying him."

Colin was stunned at Lani's conviction, to say the least. Her unwavering loyalty shocked him, especially when he'd done nothing to deserve it.

What would she want from him in return?

Pushing away from the wall, he stepped into Claudia's office. Ignoring his secretary's flush of shame, he met Lani's gaze, which turned joyful at the sight of him.

"I was hoping I'd find you here," she said, rounding the desk and coming toward him. With that unnerving habit she had, she touched him, reached for his hands. She came up on tiptoe and, as if they were alone, she brushed her lips over his.

At the touch of her mouth, his body jerked in surprise. And instant arousal.

But beyond that was another confusion. There were no recriminations from her. Not a word about the fact that he'd stayed at work to avoid her, and yes, that's exactly what he'd done.

She was smiling at him, just a sweet, simple smile. No tears, no pouting, nothing to indicate she was annoyed at him for disappointing her.

Shelly, his ex-wife, would have skinned him alive for far less.

"Will you come home with me now?" Lani murmured, looking deep into his eyes. She cupped his face, stroked his jaw with her long fingers, all in front of an avidly curious Claudia. "It's late, and I want you all to myself for this last night before your family comes."

He stared at her, having trouble putting thoughts together with her hands on him, her gaze holding his, promising things that he couldn't remember why he didn't want. "Lani—" She'd forgotten again, dammit, that this was all pretense. "Lani, this isn't—"

"You're absolutely right," she said smoothly, smiling as she stepped back and shot Claudia a laughing, sheepish look. "This isn't the place to talk like that. I'm sorry Claudia, sometimes we get carried away."

"That's okay," Claudia said, gaping.

"I'm going to take my future husband home now, for a little privacy."

Claudia shut her mouth carefully. "Well. Have a good night."

But as Lani took Colin's hand and led him out of the office, Claudia shot her boss a reassessing sort of look.

Colin wasn't sure if she was shocked that he'd let Lani lead him away, or if it had been the kiss.

Definitely the kiss he decided, rubbing the heart that was still threatening to explode out of his chest.

With her hand still holding his, Lani tugged gently, not saying another word or even looking at him as she opened the front door of the building and brought him out into the warm night.

Above them stars twinkled in the sky. The storm of the night before might never have happened. He might never have held this slight, charming, far-too-cheerful woman in his arms.

But he had, and the knowledge of her sweet, delectable body would be with him forever.

"Will you follow me back to your house?" she asked, apparently oblivious to his discomfort.

Forever.

"Colin." Lani shook her head at his silence. "This is difficult."

He shook off his reverie. "What?"

"You trying to figure out if I'm acting or if I've forgotten our deal."

"You kissed me."

"For Claudia's sake. Remember? She doesn't miss much and she needed to know we're crazy about each other."

"You were pretending?" He couldn't possibly be disappointed. Could he?

"That's the idea, right? Pretend?"

The kiss, the one that had both wowed and warmed him, hadn't been real. He laughed a little at his own stupidity. "Uh...yeah. Pretend. That's the idea."

"I came to get you because this is our last night, and we have stuff to go over."

"I know."

"I wasn't sure if you remembered."

"I remembered."

She nodded, dragged her teeth over her lower lip. Despite the warm air, she wrapped her arms around herself and stared at the mountain peaks surrounding them. The moon was nearly full, and it bounced a silvery light over the dark night. "I'm sorry," she whispered, staring at the sky. "This is awkward and I didn't want it to be. I know you overheard my conversation with Claudia."

"I'm everything she said I was."

She whipped around to face him, her eyes fierce. "You're not! You're kind and decent and sweet—"

"I think you're confusing me with Mr. Rogers and his friendly neighborhood."

Anger shot off her in waves as she lost the temper he didn't even know she had. Hair wild, eyes sparking, she came close enough to stab him in the chest with her finger. "Just because you're a private man doesn't mean you're a selfish, cold, hardhead."

"I don't remember Claudia calling me a selfish, cold, hardhead."

Some of her temper faded. "Maybe I added that."

He had to laugh.

She sighed. Shoved at her hair. Stared at him. "Tell me about you, Colin. I feel so in the dark."

"There's nothing to tell."

"Why are you such a private man? Who hurt you?"

"No one."

"I know someone did," she said softly. "I can see flashes of anguish behind that aloofness you show to everyone else. Won't you tell me about it?"

This was why he wanted everyone to think he was engaged, so he wouldn't have to ever talk about, or even *think* about, what had happened to him.

"I understand pain," she whispered, stepping close again, but instead of stabbing him with her finger, she slid a hand over his chest, down his arm to his hand, which she held in hers. "You could tell me anything."

"No. I can't." Not only was it stupid, it would be as embarrassing as hell to admit the mistakes he'd made. He'd like to think he would never do it again. And though that meant not ever trusting another woman in his life, when this woman had such pretty, trusting eyes, it was a decision he'd made out of self-preservation. He wouldn't change. "Your knowing isn't necessary for this charade of ours."

"Sharing parts of each other has nothing to do with the charade. It's part of being friends."

God, no. Being friends meant caring, genuine affection. A closeness he couldn't handle. "I'm not sure being friends is a good idea."

She stared at him for a moment, then with all traces of warmth gone from her eyes, she nodded. "I see."

It was over. He'd gone too far. But she didn't say anything. "Still want to go through with this?" he forced himself to ask.

"Yes, I do." She managed a smile at his start of surprise, though it held little mirth. "I told you, Colin, I won't go back on my word. Maybe one of these days you'll believe me. Can we go home now? It's late and I have a long day tomorrow."

Home. Their pretend home. Suddenly Colin wished, just for a second, that she was coming home with him for real. Coming to his bed. To his open arms.

"Colin?" She was waiting. "Okay?"

"Yeah." He sighed and shook off the strange yearnings. They had no place in his life. "Let's go."

THE NEXT DAY, Lani's mind wasn't much on work. Because of that, she was thankful to have a complete staff. She never left her office.

Things were good, or they would have been, if her mind hadn't kept wandering, gravitating, toward the tall, dark, enigmatic man she had agreed to help.

It wasn't Colin's fault that she wanted more. She had no one to blame for that but herself.

To combat her restlessness, she worked like a fiend, catching up on bookkeeping, phone calls and scheduling.

But she never stopped thinking about what had happened the night before.

Or rather, what *hadn't* happened.

Colin had slept in his room and she in hers. She had lain there in her big, empty chilly bed, staring at the ceiling all night, hoping the stubborn man down the hall was getting no more rest than she was.

She wondered what made him so damn unyielding. So incapable of giving in to the yearning in his heated eyes? He could deny it all he wanted, but she'd seen it for herself when she'd come out of the bathroom dressed for bed in nothing more than a plain T-shirt that hung to her thighs.

Cool, inscrutable Colin had taken one look and come to an abrupt stop. His gaze had run slowly down the length of her, lingering in spots that had made him swallow hard before dragging it back up to meet hers.

There'd been such hunger there, Lani's knees had quivered and, never one to hold back, she had actually taken a step toward him. But before she could say a word, Colin had spun on his heels and shut himself in his bedroom. Alone.

She shut off her computer now and looked out the narrow window her office afforded. It was late enough in the afternoon that she could pretend the day was over. The heat would be intense, but Colin's house was cool.

He'd be there today. He would have to be, to let in his mother and two aunts. Just thinking about it made her sweat. They were pathetically unprepared. They'd accomplished little in the past few days. Fact was, she knew no more about Colin now than when she had started this farce.

Oh, he wanted her, she knew that much about him.

She hadn't mistaken the look in his eye, the almost palpable attraction radiating between the two of them.

But for whatever reason, he refused to act on it, or even acknowledge the existence of their chemistry.

It wasn't much to go on as far as engagements were concerned.

Apparently it would have to be enough.

IT WASN'T DIFFICULT to talk herself into running errands before going to Colin's house. Lani wasn't too eager to face his mother and lie about their engagement.

She drove through town, melting in the heat, going to the bank, the gas station, the library, any place she could think of.

Then she drove to her apartment, where she grabbed her two plants. By the time she'd set them in her car, along with a few more changes of clothes, she was a sticky wreck and wishing she'd had her car air-conditioning fixed instead of paying down her credit card bill.

Out of errands and with nowhere else to go, Lani crossed the train tracks. Immediately the quality of the houses improved. Within two minutes she was heading up the steep grade that led to the hill above the town where the wealthy residents lived.

At the top of the hill, she pulled into Colin's driveway and took a long moment to admire the beautiful place. She could only imagine how wonderful it could be if Colin turned it into a real home. She glanced down at her plants. "You'll be a start," she decided. "A good start."

She let herself out of the searing hot air and into the soothing coolness of Colin's kitchen. Because her nerves were suddenly leaping, she called out jokingly, "Hi honey, I'm home!"

Juggling her plants, her purse, a bag of clothes and a smile, it took her a moment to realize she was the only one grinning.

Colin was standing at the open refrigerator, a dark eyebrow cocked. *"Honey?"*

"It's supposed to be funny."

"Ah. Well, they're in the living room, you can drop the show." He shut the refrigerator and came toward her, looking far more handsome and cool and relaxed than any man with a panicked fiancée in one room and a nosy mother in another should. He wore those jeans that made her light-headed and a dark knit polo shirt, untucked. Simple clothes. Complicated man.

Lani set down her things and took the bottled water he handed her, gratefully running the bottle over her hot forehead. *What was she going to say to his family?* Would she convince them? "Thanks," she said lightly. "Whew, it's a scorcher, isn't it?"

"What's all this?" He looked at her plants as if they held the plague.

"I know they're drooping," she said a little defensively, stroking one sagging leaf. "But they're just hot. I thought your kitchen window would be perfect for them. All that empty space."

That unsettling gaze of his switched to her, and for once he wasn't so difficult to read.

He was afraid she was forgetting again.

"You know," she said evenly, holding on to her temper. "That's getting annoying."

"This is just—"

"*Temporary*," she finished for him, rolling her eyes. "Look, are you going to remind me of that every single moment of every day?"

"Just until I'm sure you remember," he murmured, taking the water bottle from her fingers and opening it for her. Gently he brought it to her lips where she took a long, grateful sip. "You look hot."

"I brought more clothes. Is that going to scare you, too?"

"I'm not scared of you."

The heat really wasn't good for her disposition. Nor was looking at him all calm and collected while she was still sticky as hell and feeling as though she was dissolving. "Could have fooled me."

"Lani, my mother is *here*. In the next room. Are you going to do this or not?"

That was it. She didn't know if it was the temperature or just Colin annoying her all to hell, but her patience was gone. "I keep telling you I'm not going to back out! Jeez, you think you can't trust anyone."

His eyes flashed with warning, but she was good and hot and hungry, all things which had her spoiling for a fight. "No matter how grumpy and difficult you are, Colin—"

"I'm not grumpy, *you* are."

"Let's not go there, all right? I'm not going to leave you hanging. Got it?"

"Fine," he bit out. "And I'm ever so grateful." At her rough laugh, he gritted his teeth. "But if you're not going to back out, why do you keep baiting me?"

"Because you're easy."

He stared at her. "I'm— What the hell does that mean?"

"Nothing." It was irrational, but desire flooded Lani at Colin's frustration. He honestly didn't understand, or trust, her loyalty. It was infuriating. "You might have come up with a solution to your problem, Colin, namely, *me*. But I'm not some puzzle you can solve and then just forget about."

He blinked. "Are you speaking English?"

She threw up her hands. "You're impossible."

They were nose to nose now, and Lani had to admit she was enjoying the sparks flying from his eyes, because while they'd started out full of temper, they'd gone to something much hotter.

"I have feelings," she whispered. "And you have the singularly annoying ability to hurt them."

He put his big hands on her shoulders, squeezed lightly and drew her up close. "I have feelings, too."

"I never meant to hurt you." Her voice had lowered, gone husky, but she couldn't help it. The very tips of her breasts brushed his chest and suddenly she was much, much hotter.

So was he, given the low, harsh breath he let out.

"Colin...about the other night."

"When you had your dream."

"Yes." She licked her suddenly dry lips. "I don't suppose it's asking too much to know if you...uh, if you've...you know, changed your mind about going to the store?"

"For?"

"Supplies?"

He actually blushed.

"*You're* embarrassed?" she asked, shaking her head. "I'm the one that can't even say...*you know*."

"Condoms?"

Now she blushed. "Yeah."

He ran his thumb over her lower lip, mesmerized at the movement. "I went to the store."

All sorts of wicked, inappropriate thoughts danced in her head. Anticipation tingled through her body, but he sounded less than thrilled. "You didn't want to."

"No, but it wasn't my brain doing the thinking at the time."

As he spoke, their bodies touched and an electrical current ran through them.

"Is that a bad thing?" she asked. "Not thinking with your brain?"

He made a little sound, a growl of both frustration and reluctant pleasure. "It's damn suicidal. We're so attracted to each other, Lani. It's out of control. It's crazy." He sucked in a hoarse sigh when she toyed with the sensitive skin behind his ear. "Stop it." He captured her hands in his and held them between their bodies, his expression nearing pain. "It is hot in here, dammit. The air isn't working."

"It's *us*, Colin. I'm making you hot, just as you're doing the same to me. Why can't you admit that?"

"*Pretend*. The key word here, remember? This is supposed to be pretend."

"Well you can't plan everything, every little detail, for your entire life. Some things just don't work that way." He still held her hands captive. But he looked so miserable, so baffled by what was happening between them. She just had to touch him. She reached up and nipped at his jaw with her mouth.

He groaned. "Dammit, stop."

She couldn't, she felt different when she was with him. She felt good. Happy. And she knew he could feel the same way if he let himself.

What held him back?

She dragged an open-mouthed kiss down his neck, inhaling deeply his wonderful, masculine scent.

Again, he let out a rough sound of desire and helplessly pressed his hips to hers, hard. "Lani."

"Don't fight it anymore, Colin."

He stilled, then lifted his head and looked at her. His struggle to control his feelings was obvious. He harbored some secret pain and she wanted to share it.

"What the hell am I going to do with you?" he wondered.

Keep me, was on the tip of her tongue. "Kiss me," she whispered instead, leaning closer. "Kiss me like you did the other night."

He let out a rough groan and dropped his forehead to hers. "That's going to make it worse."

"I don't see how."

"Lani, don't you get it? I don't want to want you."

"Well that's a fine thing to say to your future wife."

Colin groaned again as his mother came into the kitchen.

7

IRENE WEST was a cool, calm, beautiful, five-foot-tall sophisticate. She wore expensive-looking black tailored trousers, a matching blouse so fine and shimmery smooth it had to be made of silk, and squeaky-clean, bright white tennis shoes. The latter immediately endeared her to Lani's heart.

Irene had elegant features and very chic blond hair, cut artfully to chin length. She looked unapproachable, until she smiled like a pixie.

Lani decided she was going to like her.

And what Irene said next sealed that fact.

"Kiss your fiancée, Colin," Irene instructed. "Don't make her ask you twice, it's not gentlemanly."

Lani grinned and tipped up her face.

Colin let out one concise, pithy word, shoved his fingers through his hair and glanced upward as if hoping for divine intervention.

"With sentiments like that one," Irene said disapprovingly, "you'll lose her before you ever get down the aisle. And I'm very much looking forward to that so don't blow it for me. Introduce us, Colin."

He sighed heavily, but did so, after firmly setting Lani away from him. Lani watched him slip his hands into his pockets and knew a surge of satisfaction.

He didn't trust himself not to touch her.

Even if that urge to touch was really a need to strangle her, she'd take it as a good sign.

Without a shy bone in her body, Irene smiled warmly at Lani. "I'm so happy to meet you." Her eyes held exasperated affection when she turned her fond smile on Colin. "I was becoming more and more certain I would never have the pleasure."

"You weren't going to give up until you did," Colin said dryly.

"Well somebody had to see to your happiness. I would have labored until doomsday, if needed."

Colin shot Lani a look that said, *see why we're doing this?*

Lani smiled. She thought it was cute and touching how important Colin was to Irene. But she was also beginning to understand Colin's desperate measures to ensure his privacy.

She waited for mother and son to hug, but strangely enough, they didn't. This disturbed Lani, because one of the things she remembered and missed most about her family was the physical affection.

Moving close enough to grasp Irene's hand, Lani

wrapped an arm around the woman and gave a light squeeze. "Very lovely to meet you."

"Oh," Irene whispered softly, touching Lani's face gently. "You're so sweet."

Colin frowned.

Irene ignored her son and the silent, unmistakable tension between him and Lani, her sharp yet eager eyes frankly devouring her future daughter-in-law.

Feeling a little bit on display, Lani was painfully aware of the picture she made. Self-consciously, she stroked her wild hair, trying unsuccessfully to tame it, wishing she'd combed it through. She wore little or no makeup and grungy clothes. She'd not dressed for this. For one thing, she didn't have anything suitable. And secondly, she hadn't thought of it. Why hadn't this scene occurred to her? In all her justifying of *why* she was helping Colin, in all her denials that this was nothing more than wanting to see his project completed, she'd never pictured an actual meeting with his family.

Somehow, she'd thought she would have more time. More preparation.

Actually, Lani admitted, she hadn't wanted to think about it, hadn't wanted to wonder if she'd be accepted, if she'd fit in.

Would his mother approve? After all, Lani was nothing more than a housecleaner, without social standing. She knew Colin had grown up with class and money. He'd probably had a maid, a nanny, a cook, and she'd had nothing but her great-aunt Jennie and the occasional séance.

Uncomfortable, she tugged at her ragged T-shirt, stroked a hand down her rough overalls. And wished with all her might for elegant sophistication.

"Did you work today?" Irene asked her politely.

The woman's gaze easily met Lani's and, though there was no censure there, Lani still felt it. She knew Irene was far too cultured to let her true feelings show, and certainly she had to have feelings about her son marrying someone like Lani. For the first time in Lani's life, shame filled her at her choice of a career. "Yes, I did."

Irene's features softened. Her smile was warm. "Well then you must be very tired. And here I am keeping you on your feet."

Surprise hit Lani first, then such an overwhelming gratitude she felt her eyes sting. How easy it would be to pretend this *was* real, that she really cared about what Colin's mother thought of her. But it wasn't, and it never would be. She had a job to do—convince this woman that she loved her son. Then get out of Colin's life. He would be free of hassles and she would be free to get on with her own life, happy and secure in the knowledge that she'd both helped mankind and had taken a risk for the first time in too long.

But the pathetic truth was she *did* care, about both Colin *and* what his mother thought. There was nothing she could do to stop it, not when her heart had already made the decision.

Irene pushed Lani into a chair and softened the wordless demand by saying kindly, "Would you like some iced tea?"

Colin was watching her, his eyes back to their inscrutable depths. What was he thinking? she wondered wildly. Was he worried she would fail?

Was he sorry he'd ever recruited her in the first place?

"Yes, please," she said to Irene. "But I can get it."

"No, please, let me," Irene insisted.

She looked at Colin when his mother turned her back to get the tea, fussing at her clothes, pushing at her hair, desperate for a sign that she was doing okay.

Colin's long arm reached out and gently, almost tenderly, he tucked a stray strand of hair behind her ear. His lips softened, so did his eyes, and he whispered for her ears alone, "I like the way you look, all flustered and mussed up."

Torn between pleasure at his words—*he liked the way she looked?*—and horror that she looked mussed, she bit her lip.

Colin laughed softly. "Stop it. You look..."

Their gazes met.

His breath caught.

So did hers. "I look...?"

"So pretty," came his soft, husky voice, so silky and light it felt like an embrace.

Startled, Lani blushed. "I...do?"

"Lemon in your tea, Lani?" Irene whirled back from the refrigerator. She smiled at the sight of Colin clearly doting on Lani.

"Please," Lani managed, her gaze never leaving Colin's. "Lemon would be great."

Colin didn't smile. His eyes gave nothing away except for that flash of recognition of what stood between them.

She wanted to touch him again, assure herself he was really there and for a little while, hers.

What was happening? This wasn't just a physical yearning, it went much deeper. And suddenly, the truth hit her. She wasn't capable of making up the feelings that he required for this silly pretense, not when the feelings were becoming real.

As if he could read her disturbing thoughts, Colin's eyes shuttered against her. He leaned back against the counter, his rugged body moving with easy, economical grace.

Oblivious to the arrow-taut tension between them, Irene was a study in movement, never standing still as she got a tray, some glasses, sliced a lemon and continued to talk without a breath. "I can only imagine how overwhelming this all is to you, Lani. Getting married! My, there's just so much to do, so much to think about. I hope you'll let me and my sisters help you, we just can't wait."

Colin, still watching Lani, finally let a smile touch his lips. "Did I mention how wildly enthusiastic my mother would be? Let's hope she tells the entire world so everyone will be sure to stop calling and telling me I need a date."

"Oh, you," Irene shook her head. "Stay out of this. I'm having a talk with my future daughter-in-law."

Maybe it was the title, or it might have been the sincere, warm, fondness in which Irene spoke, but at his mother's bubbly happiness, Colin's smile slowly faded.

It was replaced by worry, guilt, regret. And Lani felt every one of those emotions as well.

"I've so looked forward to this," Irene said, laughing.

Colin actually winced at that, and, at his obvious misery at having to lie, Lani's heart ached.

She reached for his hand. At the touch, he jerked in response, but he didn't pull away. She considered that great progress. "It's lovely that you came to visit, Mrs. West—"

"Oh, but you mustn't sound so formal! Please, call me Irene." She tossed a grin over her shoulder and looked twenty years younger. "Or Mom, if you think you can manage."

Mom. How many years had she wished for such a woman in her life? To be so freely given one now, when it was all just a hoax, seemed cruel. Sitting there between Colin, the man of her dreams, and his mother, a sweet, kind woman so full of heart, Lani wasn't sure she could pull it off.

"It's almost too good to believe." Irene was watching them closely. "Are you sure you're going to marry my son?"

"I—" Startled by the question, Lani looked at Colin. *She'd promised.* This predicament was her own doing now. But to out-and-out lie.... She'd not imagined how it would make her feel. "Yes, I want to marry your son," she said, and to Lani's relief, Irene accepted that.

"Good." Satisfied, Irene turned back to the counter.

It was hard to think with the weight of the lie dragging at her. Some of her happiness drained. Colin lifted her chin with a finger, looking deeply into her eyes with gratitude, and for the life of her, she couldn't turn away.

"Mom," he said quietly, still watching Lani, "I know you just got here, but I really need a moment alone with Lani."

"Oh! Of course." Irene smiled slyly as she wiped her hands on a towel. "She just got home and you haven't seen her all day. What was I thinking? I understand what young love is like." With a dramatic sigh, her expression turned dreamy. "And I can't tell you how wonderful it is to know that you've found that kind of true passion, Son."

The remorse and sorrow on Colin's face matched that in Lani's heart. How could they continue to do this? How could they lie to this woman?

"Well at least I know I can stop trying to help you find it," Irene said. "I can't tell you what a relief that is to me."

"Or me," Colin murmured.

Irene backed to the door, watching them with such affection that Lani felt like slime. "I'll just run upstairs and tell Bessie and Lola you're here." She grinned again. "My sisters are dying to meet you."

"Can you hold them off a few minutes?" Colin asked. He gestured to Lani. "I need—"

"Oh, Colin." Irene sighed wistfully, her hand over her heart. "Just to hear you say it. That you *need*. It's so beautiful. I've never known you to need anyone at all, not me, not your father, not friends or even a woman. You've always been so self-sufficient."

And alone, Lani thought. Could she fix that for him? Could she teach him the joys of true love, even when she didn't know them herself?

Irene turned to Lani. "In just a few short moments, you've given me such pleasure, you'll never know."

"I'm glad," Lani whispered, guilt tugging at her.

"Oh, we're going to have the most wonderful time." Irene's eyes lit up. "We'll throw you an engagement party next weekend. Of course, everyone will come."

Colin looked decidedly *not* excited. "Wait a minute—"

"No, don't thank me, darling." She grinned. "I insist." Then she was gone.

The silence in the kitchen was deafening.

Colin made no move to break it. Feeling awkward and uncertain, Lani moved around the table. She lifted her pathetic-looking plants and arranged them in the window.

Silly as it was, the kitchen instantly seemed homier. Happier. She hoped they lived.

Behind her, Colin still didn't speak.

The quiet grew until she couldn't stand it. "I'm sorry," she said finally.

"She's going to get hurt. *Dammit*." Colin paced the length of the kitchen, eating up the wide open space with his long, restless legs.

"Well, what did you think would happen?"

When Colin whipped around to face her, his dismay and shock evident, she shook her head and laughed. "Come on, Colin. You must have thought about what would happen after your project was finished. About how we'd end this. How she'd feel when I go back to my life."

Back to her life. Just the words brought a melancholy she didn't want to face.

Colin looked stunned.

"You didn't," she breathed. "You, Mr. Planner, Mr. Organization. You never thought about the end."

"I only thought about getting left alone." He looked disgusted with himself. "And having the phone calls stop. Ending the parade of blind dates." He swore softly before looking at her miserably. "This can't go on. I can't do it. Not to her and not to you."

"I'm okay, Colin."

"It's not fair."

He was going to call it all off. And she'd have to go back to being...without him. "You can't tell her now," she said much more casually than she felt. "It's too late. She'll get hurt either way, Colin. You might as well finish your project."

"I'm so close," he said wistfully. "So close."

Though she was beginning to understand that there would always be a project for Colin, each more important than the last, she accepted that. "The pretense is set," she said quietly. "You need time for yourself, and now you've got it. I'll keep them busy while they're here over the next few weeks. You just work as hard as you can, and get your project done. We'll face what happens afterward later."

His eyes were like the sea, black and fathomless. "Are you really up for this?"

He was talking about *them*. About what they

would have to do to pull it off. "I'm ready if you are."

A rare laugh escaped him. "Oh, I'm ready," he assured her. "But not for my project."

"No? What then?" Was that her voice, all breathless?

"The supply of condoms I bought. They're waiting upstairs by my bed."

"How many is a supply?"

He laughed again, a wondrous sound. "I got the huge economy box, thinking even that couldn't possibly be enough for the two full weeks."

Heat spiraled through her. "Oh."

"Are you sure, Lani?" His voice was low, thrilling. He came close, but didn't touch her. "Because if you're not, you'd better tell me now so I can come up with some reason why we'd be sleeping in two separate beds. I thought I could lie next to you and sleep, but I was fooling myself. We're like fire together, one touch from you and I'll go up in flames."

His voice alone was turning her on, making her tremble. "Colin, you're making my head spin."

"Well, you should see what you're doing to me."

She looked, then blushed furiously. "Oh, my."

"I've been like this since your nightmare."

Oh, my. She lifted her hands in a helpless gesture. "I haven't a clue what to do with you."

"Well that makes two of us."

LANI MET Aunt Bessie and Aunt Lola and was immediately charmed by their nosy, meddling, sweet, imposing ways. They were funny, wild, brutally honest and impossibly curious about the woman who had agreed to marry the nephew they all thought of as their own.

They ate together, and immediately afterward, Irene invited Colin to leave so he could go and work.

He hesitated, clearly torn between his unwillingness to leave Lani alone in their clutches, and the wonderful draw of his work.

But Lani knew he felt hopelessly behind on the project, so she took mercy on him and waved him off.

Besides, how was she going to learn more about him from his family while he listened to every word?

Irene, Bessie and Lola obliged her curiosity, regaling her with hysterical and interesting tales of Colin's youth.

And yet she found her attention wandering.

Would he really make love to her tonight? She wondered, glancing up the stairs in a state of high anticipation.

Oh, she hoped so.

They sat in the air-conditioned living room, a room that definitely needed a homey touch, Lani thought. There was elegant, expensive furniture, but just the bare minimum. A couch, a lamp, two chairs that looked sophisticated but uncomfortable. Not a comfy touch in sight.

She could easily fix that, with just a few plants, a nice rug, a couple of pictures.

"So you've snagged our Colin." Aunt Bessie—a four-foot-ten dynamo with the soft sweet voice of an angel and the ferocity of a protective momma bear—smiled, drawing Lani out of her reverie. "We're so thankful, darling, really we are." She leaned forward conspiratorially. "But do you think you could tell us *why?*"

"Why?" Lani blinked. Had she missed something?

"Why you want him."

Eager, Lola and Irene leaned forward, too. "He's such a pain in the tushie," Lola commented, her voice full of exasperated love. "We just want to know how you bullied him into it again."

It took her a moment to switch gears from putting warm, soft touches on the house to... "*Again?*" Lani straightened, her full attention focused now. "I'm sorry. Did you say, again?"

"Why, yes." Lola didn't move. She was the tallest at five foot two, and skinny as a rail. Her voice was husky, deep and loud. "We're dying to know how you convinced him to try again, when for five years we've been so unsuccessful."

"I see." Lani nodded calmly while her head spun. "He's been married before."

"Uh-oh." Bessie sat back and bit her meddling lip. "Oh, dear. Dear, dear, dear. Irene...?"

Irene glared at both her sisters. "Now you've done it." She turned to Lani with a worried smile. "Lani—"

"He's been married before," she repeated like a parrot. All the signs had been there, of course. His reluctance to share himself. His fear of being hurt. Still, devastation rocked her.

"Damn!" Lola cried. "We blew it!"

"*We?*" Irene demanded, sitting upright with dignity. "I am not going down for this. No way. I should have left the two of you in New York!"

"Well how was I supposed to know she didn't know?" Lola asked. "Somebody tell me that."

"We should have known," Bessie decided. "Colin always has been so closed-mouthed. It's natural that he wouldn't tell her about his single-most devastating failure."

"Wait a minute." Lani tried again to soak this all in. "Give me a minute here. Colin's been...*married.*" She looked at them, feeling weak. "How could I not have figured that out by now?"

But the argument between the sisters was in full swing.

"I knew better than to bring the two of you with me," said Irene. She glared at her sisters. "I told you, *let me handle it. Let me check out the fiancée for myself,* but no, you both had to come. You had to interfere. Now look what you've done!"

"No offense, Sissy," Bessie interrupted stiffly. "But I was more Colin's mother than you ever were, so I had the right to meet Lani first."

Irene stood, then, quivering with indignation. "Now, just a minute—"

Bessie stood, too, glaring. "Yes?"

Good Lord, the three of them, these elegant socialites, were going to brawl. "Ladies..."

"You might think Colin belongs to you, but he's mine. *Mine*," Irene emphasized. "That means Lani is mine, too!"

"Okay, that's it. *Stop*." Lani stood up from the circular sofa, where they were perched in front of the lovely fireplace she'd had such high hopes for. "It's true then, he's really already been...married?"

Silence fell while all three older women shifted uncomfortably.

"It's really a very simple question," Lani said calmly as if her heart hadn't just cracked. She had a terrible feeling she now had the answer to the secret anguish swimming in Colin's eyes.

Was he pining away for a woman who'd left him?

Had the ex broken his heart, causing him never to trust another?

And how in the world could Lani compete with such a memory? The answer was simple. She couldn't. "Please tell me."

Irene sighed but looked right at Lani. "Yes, Colin was married before. I'm sorry you didn't know. Even sorrier that you had to find out like this, from us."

It took Lani a minute to collect herself; she felt such sorrow, both for her and for Colin. But she wasn't a selfish person by nature, and after the first fling of self-pity had passed, she hurt only for Colin. To know how much he must have loved his ex-wife, so much that he couldn't allow himself to have a real home or family now, was unbearably sad.

Somehow she managed to excuse herself.

They let her go, their eyes sad and worried, but she couldn't reassure them. Not yet.

She went straight to Colin's office upstairs, planning on opening her arms and her heart, wanting to tell him how sorry she was about his past. She wanted to share whatever comfort she could. Surely she could help, now that she understood.

But he was gone.

She assumed he had gone to his other office, the one in town. Disappointed, she climbed the stairs, walked into his bedroom and got ready for bed. She'd wait.

Feeling a little bit like Goldilocks, she climbed into his huge, soft, welcoming bed.

And waited.

The sheets smelled like him. The room looked like him. She felt him all around her. She daydreamed about what would happen, how she'd help heal him and, in return, he'd take her to ecstasy.

Sighing, imagining his body, his hands, his mouth, all on her, she sank down into the covers and waited some more.

And waited. And waited.

Only, Colin never came, and finally, exhausted, Lani fell asleep, his pillow hugged tight to her body.

8

GETTING LOST in his work was the last thing Colin had expected to do, especially with thoughts of Lani dancing through his head, but by the time his thoughts switched from work to life, it was 2:00 a.m. How had that happened? Hours had passed.

Lani would be waiting for him.

She'd be warm and inviting, he imagined, *smiling as she lifted her arms to welcome him.*

Wrong.

It was the middle of the night. She'd be asleep, and if she wasn't, she'd be mad as hell. Rightly so.

Racing home, he found her pretty much as his wildest fantasies had dictated, sprawled on the bed. There was one difference however. She wasn't hot and bothered, instead she was fast asleep with her arms squeezing his pillow close to her heart.

Damn, he'd really blown it. He had to have hurt her feelings again, and he hated that. Much as he loved his work, right then and there he experienced a first—a spurt of genuine anger at how it consumed him body and soul, to the point of such forgetfulness.

He had to make it up to her, had to at least apologize. "Lani?"

It didn't help that the sheets and blanket had become tangled in her legs, below her hips. She wore a tiny white camisole that looked soft and silky, and even tinier panties. Her skin was pale and creamy and glowed in the faint moonlight.

She took his breath away.

Helplessly drawn to where she lay, he kneeled on the mattress. "Lani?"

In her sleep, she frowned, and from deep in her throat came a low sound of irritation.

Still Colin leaned over her, hand outstretched, hoping to wake her, planning on starting with sweet, sexy promises.

But then he was stopped cold, frozen by the tracks of dried tears on her cheeks.

THE NEXT MORNING Colin was back in his office downtown, unable to concentrate on a damn thing except Lani and how she'd looked in his bed.

As if she belonged there.

The long restless night on his floor, listening to Lani's soft, deep breathing, hadn't improved his disposition.

"Line one's for you." From the door, Claudia thrust her chin at his phone. "The Institute."

"Great," he said, meaning anything but. He had

nothing new to report. He still wasn't finished and wasn't sure when he would be. "Claudia?"

She'd turned away and was halfway out the door when he said her name. She stiffened, but didn't look at him. "Yeah?"

"Next time you want to scare off a woman for me, can you check and make sure it's one I want scared off?"

"God." She winced and turned back to face him, her expression full of guilt. "I'm so sorry! I'm so used to trying to chase off everyone your mother sets you up with, I didn't realize she was the real thing."

The real thing. His stomach hurt. "Has word gotten around?"

She smiled. "Oh, yeah. Women from all over the county are having a wake in honor of your lost single status. You're the talk of the town. So is Lani." A slight frown marred her face. "She's really wonderful, you know."

He was beginning to realize that. "I know."

"Loyal, dedicated. Sweet, too, and very kind."

"But?" Colin pushed away his work. It held little appeal at the moment. "I'm sure I heard one at the end of that sentence."

"Well..." Claudia sent him an apologetic look to soften her words. "Truth is, I think she's *too* wonderful for you. She'll want more than you'll give her, Colin."

"And what would that be?" he said, amused now.

"I have more money than I know what to do with, a huge house with every amenity she could ever want. There's nothing missing. I can give her whatever she needs."

Claudia's look turned pitying. "See? That's *exactly* what I mean. You don't have a clue as to how to keep a woman like that." She gave him a long look that made him squirm. "Or maybe you do, and you just don't want to see it."

"I have a call," he said, conveniently remembering. He picked up the phone, almost forgetting that this whole thing was just a sham. That he didn't have to justify anything to his secretary. That it didn't really matter what anyone thought because what he had with Lani was just temporary.

Temporary.

But before he pressed in the phone line, he watched Claudia shake her head in disgust, watched her leave...and knew she spoke the truth.

He didn't have a clue as to how to keep a woman like Lani. *Any* woman.

And he had an ex-wife to prove it.

COLIN GLARED at his office phone. He hadn't been able to reach Lani all day, either at the house or at her office.

Had she bolted, tired of the charade?

He couldn't blame her, but hoped not, and not because he'd have nothing to tell his interfering mother and aunts. He just couldn't leave things between them as they were now.

It was only three in the afternoon, an hour of the day he rarely saw because he usually had his head buried in work, but he actually got up and left his office. At the moment, he couldn't have buried himself in his work to save his sorry life, and he had Lani's huge, expressive eyes to thank.

He couldn't get them out of his mind. How was she feeling about last night?

All he'd ever wanted was peace and quiet. He'd never wanted to hurt anyone; not his family and certainly not Lani.

How he had managed to get himself in such trouble was beyond him.

He drove up to her apartment, once again struck by the differences in their life-styles. He walked up the cracked, crumbling driveway, wishing he could get Lani a better place to live. But he knew she'd never accept such help from him.

She worked so hard. It didn't seem fair that this was all she had to show for it.

"She's not here."

He turned and was surprised to see an old woman speaking to him. She was tiny, at least eighty years old, and dressed in hot-pink-and-red spandex. "Excuse me?" he said politely.

"Lani. She's who you're looking for, isn't she? Your...fiancée?"

"You know Lani?"

That made her laugh until her rust-colored curls bounced. Well, actually *cackle* would be a better word for what she did. She bent at the waist, slapped her knees and let loose. Finally, sniffing, she straightened. Still grinning, she nodded. "Yep, I know her." Grabbing a rake, she leaned against the fence of the small garden.

For the first time, Colin realized that while the apartment building itself looked as though it had seen better days, the garden was full and lush and well tended.

"The question is," the woman asked. "Do *you* know Lani?"

She was missing some marbles, Colin decided. "I'm sorry. You're...?"

"Ah, no doubt you're right. Where are my manners? We've not been introduced. Strange, wouldn't you say, since I'm Lani's great-aunt Jennie?" She eyed him shrewdly, acknowledging his surprise with a lift of a gray eyebrow.

Lani had a crazy woman for an aunt?

"I raised your soon-to-be-wife," she told him. "But, of course, you knew that, since you're engaged to her. You know everything about her. Right?"

Somehow he'd managed to step into an episode of the "X-Files."

Great-Aunt Jennie winked, then leaned close and

whispered conspiratorially, "Nice to meet you, Mr. Pretend Fiancé."

She knew.

Unperturbed by his silence, Great-Aunt Jennie made herself comfortable on a wooden bench and tapped the spot next to her.

Colin sat.

The old woman smiled, her pink-and-red workout suit glittering in the relentless sun. "Next to you, I'm all Lani has," she confided. "But you knew that already, too, right?"

He should have. That message came loud and clear.

"She loves flowers, did you know that?" Jennie asked. "She also loves loud music, kids and has a serious weak spot for kittens. And Lord, does that girl have a sweet tooth. It's amazing how good a figure she has, given what she eats. Did you know she has a particular thing for white chocolate?"

A real fiancé would know these things, and more, about the woman he loved.

He would also know where to find her on any given day.

"And I don't have to tell you her dislikes, namely vegetables and exercise," Jennie said easily. "Or that she fears violent thunderstorms because her parents died in one."

Colin remembered Lani's fear well. Terrified, she'd clutched at him every time thunder had hit. "I didn't know that," he admitted.

"You should have."

"Yes." He most definitely should have.

Sadness was etched in Jennie's every movement as she stood and dragged the rake across a few fallen leaves. "I'm sorry. I love her and I'm upset. I'm taking it out on you, and that's very unkind of me. Inexcusable actually. Please forgive me. It's not you I'm mad at, but my darling, huge-hearted, idiot niece."

"Lani's parents—"

"Died when she was six." She lifted her head and met his gaze with her own steady one. "I'm her mother and her father now and her best friend. I'm certain you're not good for her, but one of these days, I'll learn to let her make her own mistakes."

Colin could not dispel the image of Lani as a child, frightened and alone, facing her parents' death at such a young age.

"And don't bother to ask me anything else. I won't tell you." She lifted a stubborn chin, sharing a strong resemblance to Colin's equally stubborn fiancée. "Whatever you want to know, you'll have to ask her yourself."

"I will." Soon as he could find her. He stood, intending to do just that.

"Lani told me about you." When he pivoted back around, startled, Jennie set the rake aside and pierced him with sharp blue eyes. "She told me you were smart and compassionate and wonderful."

Colin blinked in surprise, but Jennie only nodded. "She's a very generous soul, my Lani."

Pride tasted like hell, but Colin swallowed it anyway. "Do you know where I could find her?"

"Depends why you want her."

Because I miss her. But because that was a ridiculous thought, he shook his head to clear it. "I'd like to talk to her."

Jennie just looked at him, smiling. Silent. Smug.

Dammit. "Okay, I hurt her feelings. I have to see her, try to talk to her about it."

She was silent for so long, Colin thought she'd fallen asleep leaning on her rake.

"She's working," she said at last. "Too hard, if you ask me."

Again, another message. But Jennie didn't understand how complicated this was. Under their present terms, Lani would never allow him to help her financially, no matter how much he'd like to. "I called her office already," he said. "She wasn't there."

"Of course not." Jennie's expression made it clear that she thought *he* was the crazy one. "She doesn't spend all day sitting behind a desk, Mr. Pretend Fiancé. Not like other people. No, she's out there working her fingers to the raw bone, cleaning *rich* people's places because they don't want to do it themselves."

Well he had to hand it to the woman. In the space

of the few minutes that he'd been there, she'd made him feel ridiculous, selfish, greedy and now guilty.

But Lani liked her work, didn't she? God, he didn't know, he'd never even asked. "I just want to talk to her. We have a lot to work out. Most of which is a direct result of my own stupidity, if you must know."

Jennie laughed loudly. "Nice to see a man admit it."

"Can you tell me where to find her? Please?"

Jennie hesitated a long moment, and Colin knew he was being seriously measured. He had no idea what Lani had told Jennie about him. Hell, up until now, he'd had no idea who made up Lani's family.

How could he not have known that? How could he not have asked?

"She'll be cleaning Dr. Morrow's offices today," Jennie said finally. "On Main Street."

"Thank you," he said sincerely, but something had him hesitating, and it took him a second to realize he wanted this woman's approval. For Lani's sake. *For his.* The feeling was so alien, he didn't know what to do with it, but he found himself saying, "I won't hurt her."

"Of course you will." Her smile was sad, and she suddenly looked much older than she had before.

When he opened his mouth to protest, she lifted a hand with a sharp shake of her head. "Don't make promises you can't keep, Colin. I know this engagement isn't real, at least not to you."

She didn't have to tell Colin what she thought of that, it was all over her face.

"Lani has talked herself into believing she's helping you," she said. "And maybe she is, but believe me, she'll get hurt. I'm not happy with you for that."

She walked back into her house, leaving Colin to his own miserable thoughts.

COLIN HAD NO TROUBLE finding Dr. Morrow's offices on Main Street. He had no trouble parking, no trouble at all walking into the building, the one with a brightly colored sign announcing that today was Dr. Morrow's day at the local hospital.

What Colin did have trouble with was figuring out what the hell he was going to say to Lani.

Or what the hell he wanted from her.

He entered the empty waiting room, figuring he'd find Lani on her hands and knees, slaving away in shapeless clothes that hardly fit her. Or maybe she'd be up on a ladder brushing away at dust bunnies, her face streaked with sweat and dirt, her hands worked red and raw.

Certainly she'd be solemn and upset over the night before.

Whatever he'd expected, it certainly wasn't to find her rosy and screaming with laughter, pointing a squirt bottle filled with water at his aunt Bessie, who was squealing in response, also wielding a water bottle like a weapon.

Behind them both, shouting like a crazed banshee, came his aunt Lola, waving yet another squirt bottle. She had a handkerchief wrapped around her head. "Duck or you die," his oldest and most dignified aunt yelled, grinning widely from ear to ear.

"What the—" he began, only to find himself the target of three wild-looking women. He registered the change in their eyes, saw the exact moment the target of their fun game switched from each other to him.

Him.

"Now wait just a minute," he said, backing up as all three women advanced on him. "Just—"

It was all he got out before Lani—not looking even close to devastated—took the lead and sprayed him full in the face.

From the couch came a strange, muffled sound. It was Carmen, working hard at reading a magazine, holding her hand over her mouth as her shoulders shook with silent laughter.

Water dripped off Colin's nose, down his ears, into his collar. Both his aunts found this absolutely hysterical. Bessie was so overcome she had to sink to one of the couches. She rolled back and forth, laughing as tears ran down her face.

Lola took one look at her and snorted in a most unladylike fashion, which sent Bessie and Lani back into fresh fits of giggles.

Colin gawked at Lani. Tears of mirth streamed down her face, along with a good amount of water—one of his aunts had obviously gotten her good. Her hair was out of control, rioting around her face, her eyes were bright, her skin positively glowing.

Nope, no matter how hard he looked, he couldn't find an ounce of solemnity about her.

She squirted him again.

"What was that for?" he sputtered as he wiped cold, wet drops from his face.

"Well..." She grinned. "You looked hot." Her smile mocked him and his all-day misery.

The urge to haul her to him and kiss away all frustration came on incredibly strong, but he couldn't be sure he wouldn't strangle her. He actually reached out to grab her, but at the last minute remembered his avidly watching, meddling aunts and slammed his hands into his pockets instead.

She'd sprayed him, right in the face! He couldn't believe it, couldn't believe how shock had turned into something else, something far more base. If he didn't kiss her right here and now, he would just explode.

The primal, savage urge startled him. He'd never, ever, felt this way over a woman. Over work, yes. But never another human, and it shook him to the core.

She wore jeans today, and while they were several sizes too large for her, hiding the figure he knew could alter his blood pressure, they had holes all over, including one high on her right thigh that revealed enough skin to have him swallowing hard.

Where was his distraught, depressed fiancée?

"What are you doing here?" she asked sweetly, as if she hadn't attacked him with a squirt bottle only a second before.

"What am *I* doing here?" He let out a sound of amazement. "I've been going crazy looking for you. What are *you* doing here?"

"It's not too difficult to figure out." She smiled innocently, gesturing to her cleaning supplies, lying useless and unused on the floor. She seemed without a care in the world. As if she hadn't given him a second thought.

She probably hasn't. The thought was curiously deflating.

"I'm working," she said. "Very hard."

"Oh, yeah, I can see that."

Lani turned slightly to glance at his aunts, and when she did, Colin's eyes nearly bugged out of his head. The back of her jeans were even holier than the front. There was a slice through the denim so high on her left thigh he could see a flash of hot-pink panties.

Had he really once thought this woman not sexy? How had he been so blind?

With Lani giving them some silent but meaningful

looks, Bessie and Lola finally managed to control themselves and straightened.

"Better get to work," Bessie said cheerfully, nudging her sister. They beckoned Carmen, who with a sniff of disdain, took her magazine, rudely stuck her tongue out at Colin, then disappeared down the hall.

Colin's aunts then grabbed a bucket full of cleaner and sponges.

"What are you doing?" he asked.

Lola and Bessie, both old enough to be grandmothers, both world travelers and grand sophisticates of the small educated, high-brow population of Sierra Summit, grinned wildly.

"Lani's short-handed today, poor thing," Lola said. "She could never get everything done all by herself so we're staff today. I'm going to clean the bathrooms."

"And I'm on vacuuming and dusting detail," Bessie said proudly.

Colin couldn't believe it. "But neither of you have cleaned a toilet or worked a vacuum in your lives."

"Always a first time, hon." Bessie's smile turned wicked, and Colin knew enough about his aunt to know he wasn't going to like what she had to say next. "And speaking of first times," she continued sweetly, "we're really short-handed here, and on a time budget since Lani pays by the hour. I think since she's your fiancée, you should help."

"*What?*"

"Grab a sponge, darling," Lola said, nodding her approval. "Let's see you prove your worth to this wonderful girl here. Give her a hand."

Colin turned to stare at Lani. "Are they kidding?"

She looked at his aunts with laughter and affection in her gaze, but when she turned back to him, she said somberly, "Nope. I don't think they are."

He thought about what he'd learned from her great-aunt Jennie, how hard she worked. How loyal and caring she was. How she'd lost her family so early.

How she feared storms.

He was beginning to realize the extent of Lani's depth and inner strength, and though he admired her very much for it, a much more basic emotion pushed to the surface.

Protectiveness.

"Unless of course, Colin, you can't spare the time for her," Bessie said evenly.

Lola shifted the bucket in her arms like a pro. "Or maybe you think pushing a sponge isn't your kind of work."

He couldn't believe it. These two women supposedly loved him as if he was their own child. Why were they giving him hell?

But they were right. He'd always put work ahead of everything else, and he'd always thought himself far above cleaning.

Guilt and shame were new to him, and he didn't

like either. "I'll help, dammit." He grabbed a sponge, but then Lani was there with a hand to his chest, her eyes soft and apologetic.

"They're just teasing you." She wiped a drop of water off his jaw. "I'm fine, I don't need you to stay."

"I said I'd help."

She looked into his eyes and apparently saw she couldn't convince him otherwise. "All right, then," she said quietly. "Thank you."

He unbuttoned his cuffs and shoved up his sleeves. "Where's my mother?"

"Florist shopping." Lani chewed on her lip in the gesture he now knew was a nervous habit.

"For the wedding," Lola added. "She's so excited. And the engagement party is completely under control. You two are going to love it."

It was all too much, and he could see in Lani's eyes she felt it, too. "We really don't need an engagement party," he said. "I wish you wouldn't go to the trouble."

"Of course you need one." Bessie rubbed her hands together in delight just thinking about it. "It'll be spectacular. Flowers, candles, music for dancing. So romantic."

"An engagement party," Lani whispered to herself, the sweet look of longing on her face tearing at Colin.

She wanted it to be real, with all her heart. Knowing that, he felt overwhelmed. What had he done to her? Hell, to *him*. For a moment he couldn't even remember why he had chased her all over town and back. He should have left it alone.

Lani was staring at him. "What did you just say?"

"Nothing."

"No, you most definitely said something." She stepped closer, studying him intensely. "You said you can't remember why you were worried about me."

Great, had he really said that out loud?

"Why were you worried, Colin?"

"You're hearing things."

"I don't think so." She was right in front of him now, smelling like pine cleaner and shampoo and he wanted badly to haul her close and show her exactly what all this insanity did to him.

"You chased me all over town? Really?"

"So?"

At that statement of brilliance, Lani let out a little smile, as if she found his rare petulance very funny.

He didn't find anything even remotely humorous about it, and this time when she took another step toward him, he backed up.

This made her eyes warm, though he had no idea why, and now in addition to the humor he could see so plainly on her face, he also saw affection and more emotion than he knew what to do with. He was painfully aware of their audience when she asked him softly, kindly, "Did you need me for something?"

He stared at her. "Yeah."

"Can you tell me what?"

"Not in mixed company."

Bessie and Lola snickered in delight and left them in peace. Finally.

Silence reigned.

With both his aunts gone, Lani's bravado seemed to fade. She clasped her hands, studied her feet, then played with a spec of dust on the floor with her toe.

"Lani..." But nothing else came out. Now that he was here, with her right there within his reach, he hadn't a clue as to what to say or do.

She solved that for him. "I'm sorry your marriage didn't work out, Colin." Her voice was quiet, full of sorrow. "I know you must have loved her very much if you haven't wanted to be in another relationship since. A *real* one anyway."

9

LANI HADN'T MEANT to just throw it out like that. She'd really intended to bring up Colin's marriage much more gently. She'd wanted him to understand that she was very sorry he'd gotten so hurt, that she understood how much he must have loved his wife.

And if irrational jealousy pounded through her, she would keep that part to herself.

But after her statement, Colin had carefully closed his mouth, grabbed a sponge and disappeared down the hallway of the medical building.

Lani had let him go. This was neither the time nor the place to hash it out, no matter how much she wanted to comfort him, wanted to encourage him to give love another shot with someone who would never hurt him, with someone who would cherish him until the end of her life.

And if she was thinking that that someone could be her, if she had conveniently forgotten she wanted no more of an emotional tangle than he did, she would live with that.

"You're an idiot," she whispered to herself, shov-

ing her hair out of her face. In one of the private patient rooms, she swept the floor with a vengeance.

"Who told you?"

She nearly dropped her broom.

"I want to know how you know," Colin said,
standing in the doorway, quietly furious.

"It doesn't matter." Her heart ached because only
a deep, unrelenting pain would cause him to be so
upset. She knew first-hand how much damage that
kind of anguish could cause. "I'm sorry you got hurt
by it, Colin. I'm sorry your heart was broken."

His jaw tightened. His eyes went hard. "I absolutely don't want to talk about it."

"But—"

"Never, Lani."

"It's not a crime to still love her."

The laugh that escaped him was short and hard.
"You've got it very wrong."

"Then tell me."

"Just leave it the hell alone."

She leaned on the broom and studied him. "You
could tell me about it, you know. I'd listen and
maybe you'd feel better."

"I've got a better idea. Let's talk about you. About
why you never tell me anything about yourself."

"You've never asked."

"Tell me about your family."

"All right. I have only my great-aunt Jennie. It's
been just us for a long time."

"Does the reason for that have anything to do with your nightmares?"

She paled, felt the blood drain right out of her face. "Yes."

"It's also probably the reason you're alone now. Just like me, you're not interested in more hurt. Am I right?"

She crossed her arms, chilled. "I don't think I want to talk about it."

"Well then, we're even, aren't we?"

Damn him for turning this around. It wasn't about her, it was about *him.* He'd never see that, not right now. "I have work."

"Yes, well so do I." And he vanished.

He'd go back to his work, she thought wearily, and bury both himself and his anguish in it, and it would be all the harder to reach him.

She figured he'd done exactly that, so when she heard the crash from the next patient room, she assumed it was Bessie, Lola or Carmen.

She went running, imagining all sorts of things, only to skid to a halt in the doorway.

On his butt, on a very wet floor, surrounded by a spilled bucket and a mop, sat Colin.

He wore a disgusted expression. Lani covered her mouth, but a laugh escaped anyway, making his frown all the more fierce.

"I suppose you think this is funny," he growled.

"Are you all right?"

He shoved to his feet. "Physically? Fine." He patted the seat of his drenched trousers. "Though my ego just took a hell of a beating."

"I'm sorry."

"Yeah? Then why are you grinning?"

Lani shook her head, but ruined it with another laugh that she quickly swallowed. "It's relief that you're okay. Honest."

"Right." He pulled at the material clinging to him.

"I thought you'd left."

"I told you I would help, dammit, and I'm going to help. I just don't want to talk while I do it."

"Then why did you come?"

"You disappeared, I was worried."

"I was working," she pointed out gently.

"I didn't know. I thought maybe you were upset or mad. Maybe you'd decided that—" Swearing, he broke off and looked away. "Never mind."

Her stomach twisted. "That I would leave? I won't, Colin. I told you that."

But she was going to have to prove it, she realized. Not only prove it, but give him the time to accept it as well. She could do that. For him, she could probably do anything.

"People don't always do what they say they're going to do," he said.

"I do." She smiled at his noncommittal grunt. "Oh, Colin. You don't have to follow me around and mop and—" she gestured with her hand to his very wet backside "—do the slip and slide just to keep me."

His eyes narrowed on her, and the laughter she'd been barely holding back escaped.

With a suddenly wicked gaze, he came slowly, purposely, toward her. "You're laughing at me, Lani. Again."

"Now, Colin—" She backed up, right into the door, which shut behind her. She held her broom between her hands like a shield. "I wasn't laughing *at* you...just *with* you."

"Uh-huh." He kept coming, this big, sleek male animal. This big, sleek, wet, *annoyed* male animal.

"It's that you're so cute," she said quickly. "Coming here, wanting to help me—"

He was there in a flash, moving far more quickly and gracefully than she'd expected, sandwiching her between the door and his body.

"I didn't realize how nice it would feel to have you care about me," she managed. Oh, he felt good, so very good, against her. "You gave up your own important work today to come here and fall on your butt—"

He held her head in his big, gentle hands, his body imprisoning hers. "Stop it."

"But it's such a great butt, Colin." She burst out into renewed laughter at his expression.

"Lani? Be quiet." Reaching around her, he flicked

the lock on the door, and with a loud, metallic sound, it slid home.

The amusement backed up in her throat, immediately replaced by a searing, heated excitement. "Colin..." Did he have any idea what that look on his face did to her insides? "Your aunts..."

"...will no doubt be listening so you'd better keep it quiet, hadn't you?" She was flattened to the door, between the hard wood and his even harder body. Gentle but inexorable fingers found the rip in the front of her jeans and played with the soft, giving skin on the inside of her thigh.

Her heart thundered in her chest. "I know you're upset because I probed into your personal life..."

Now his other hand slid around to the back of her, toying with the larger rip back there, stroking the flesh just beneath her panty line. "This has nothing to do with anyone else," he informed her, his fingers shifting slightly, playing with the elastic on her hot-pink panties.

Lani forced herself to remain absolutely still, when what she really wanted was to arch into his hand. "Then you're embarrassed about that little pratfall you took." She gasped as he slowly traced the line of the material. "But you don't have to be."

"This isn't about the fall either," he assured her roughly, slipping beneath the material now to cup her bare bottom in his hand. He kneaded it gently, sighing at the connection. "It's about before that. It's about last night and this morning and the fact I can't get you out of my head."

The words broke through her haze of passion, and they meant so much she could hardly speak. "Really? You think about me?"

"Yeah. Really."

"You don't like it."

"Not much," he admitted. "But that doesn't seem to stop me." Abruptly, he backed away from her. Shoving the bucket and mop aside with his foot, he grabbed her wrist and hauled her across the room, to the full-sized hospital bed that Dr. Morrow used to treat his patients. "Lani, I have to touch you."

"You *were* touching me."

"More then."

She couldn't breathe. "Colin, I was thinking—"

"I was, too. You should be quiet now."

She nodded. "Okay."

With a none-too-gentle push, Colin pressed her down on the mattress. The bed groaned when he followed her. Seizing the broom she still held between them, he flung it across the room.

Then his mouth took hers, hot and demanding.

The connection sizzled. Dizzy with it, Lani could only cling to him. Her heart had already been aroused, from the very moment he'd stormed into the office looking for her, so it didn't take much more than a stroke of his tongue to bring her startlingly close to completion.

He tore his mouth away and stared at her. "You're driving me crazy."

"The feeling is mutual." She had gripped his shirt in fisted hands, holding him close. She couldn't bring herself to let him go. "You were going to touch me, Colin. Why aren't you?"

He settled himself between her legs, spreading them farther to accommodate his body. He rocked against her with a slow, building rhythm that had her moaning, gasping for more, a slave to the motion.

She couldn't keep a thought in her head as her body raced desperately. Colin gripped her hips in his hands, arching them up to better meet his, his erection nestling tightly to the aching flesh between her thighs, and the friction was so delicious she could hardly stand it. His mouth trailed over her jaw to her ear. The sound of his ragged, uneven breathing assured her he was every bit as wild as she. Still fully dressed, she was going to climax, with nothing more than his hips sliding against hers.

"I don't know what's happening," he whispered, bewildered. She writhed against him and he moaned. "This was supposed to be fake, dammit."

Only a few strokes away from blessed orgasm, Lani could do nothing but hang on for dear life. "Don't stop," she begged.

"*Fake*," he repeated hoarsely, still rocking against her in perfect harmony.

Her body tightened, she couldn't see, could only feel, she was so close. He captured her mouth again, the kiss deep and urgent and so needy Lani's entire heart melted. And just to make sure she lost the rest of her head completely, he stroked his hands over her body, molding and pressing and coaxing, then slowing to kiss her again, until she was whimpering and begging and writhing beneath him.

"Lani, let me, let me—" Rearing up, he unbuttoned her cotton work shirt, letting out a groan when he found her bare beneath it. He dipped down, nuzzling first, then taking a tight, waiting nipple into his mouth. His hands went to the buttons of her jeans and while he fumbled there, she attacked his shirt, shoving her hands beneath it.

"This is crazy," he muttered, slipping his warm, rough hands into the back of her jeans. Scooping her hips up, he thrust against her again, rubbing her with the hard ridge of his erection. He let out a dark, needy sound and dropped his forehead to hers. "I can't get enough of you, I need more...."

"More," she agreed breathlessly, nearly crying in relief when she heard the rasp of his zipper. He shoved his jeans down, freeing himself. The back of his hand grazed the part of her that was hot and wet for him. Just that light brush of his knuckles was enough to send her once again skittering to the very edge. She tossed her head back as her limbs started to shake. Heat spiraled through her and she grabbed his hand, needing just one more touch to send her over, just one more little touch....

The knock at the door had them both freezing. Hot, unseeing gazes locked on each other.

"Darling?" came Bessie's voice. "We're finished in the front room. Is Lani in there with you?"

Lani loved Bessie, really she did, but at that moment, she wanted to scream and stamp her feet. She wanted to throw a full-blooded tantrum at the fate of Bessie's bad timing.

It wasn't fair! She'd been so close, so very close, that her entire body was damp and trembling and still rocking helplessly.

Above her, a solid mass of taut, quivering sexual animal, Colin growled. His shirt was shoved open, thanks to her desperate fingers. His zipper was down, his hair wild, his eyes were beyond description. His chest was hard and slick, his belly flat and rippled with strength. Below that...oh, my. He was magnificent.

And furiously aroused.

"Hello, Colin?" Bessie called. The doorknob rattled, making Lani thankful for the lock.

Colin hadn't moved, and Lani could understand. She could hardly think. She licked her lips and cleared her throat, but still her voice sounded weak and trembly. "We're both in here, Bessie," she managed. "Fighting some nasty dirt, too." She glanced at Colin. He hadn't moved or blinked. She could feel him between her spread legs, hot and throbbing. "We'll...we need a moment," she said weakly.

"No problem," Bessie called cheerfully. "We'll wait."

She let out a choked laugh. "They'll wait," she whispered up to Colin, who shook his head and groaned.

"Great," he said through clenched teeth. For a moment, he sagged over her, bracing himself on his forearms. His eyes were already shuttered, hiding himself, so it surprised her when he leaned close and brushed his lips over hers in one quick, hot, hard kiss.

"Oh, Colin," she murmured against his mouth, holding him tight.

"I know."

"I can't stand it."

"I'm going to kill them," he assured her. "*They'll wait*," he repeated with disgust, pushing off her and yanking his shirt back up over his shoulders. "Damn, they've got timing."

Lani didn't respond.

Colin turned back to her and groaned. She was still sprawled on the bed, clothes awry, hair everywhere, lips wet from his mouth, looking mouthwateringly beautiful.

He struggled to close his zipper over his still raging erection.

Lani lifted an eyebrow. "Careful with that,"

He laughed, then winced as he finally got his pants closed. What was it about her? She made him smile, made him laugh. When was the last time anyone had done that for him?

She also made him ache.

He went to her, gently took her hands and pulled her upright. The movement shifted her shirt open again, and her warm, full breasts spilled out. When he drew the material closed, he let his knuckles brush over her one last time.

She pressed against him. "I didn't want to stop," she whispered, burying her face in his neck. "I was so close!"

Carefully he sucked in both his breath *and* the urge to haul her to him. He searched hard and deep, but from nowhere within himself could he summon up the need to flinch from her affection.

He didn't understand it. They weren't having sex and yet he still wanted to hold her. It was a very new concept for him.

And a scary one.

She hadn't moved, other than to burrow into him. "Come on," he whispered, taking her shoulders and straightening her. "We have to pull it together, Lani."

"No." She let her shirt fall open again and when his eyes crossed with lust, she hummed with satisfaction, drawing him back to her. "I don't want to pull it together, I want to come apart. With you."

His hands were full of hot, sexy, needy woman, the first woman to actually attract him in far too long. In light of that, he couldn't believe he was holding her away from him, begging her to stop. "Lani, please."

"Yoo-hoo!" Lola tapped cheerfully on the door. "Lani, honey, where's the—'

"We'll be right there!" Colin bellowed. "Hurry," he whispered, drawing Lani to her feet and yanking up her jeans. "Snap them," he urged while he attempted to tuck in her shirt.

"That's the last time I ask them for their help." Irritation swam in her voice as she finally—thankfully—fastened all her clothes, hiding that gorgeous, mind-numbing body from view.

Colin smiled, not an easy feat in his condition. "I thought you liked them."

"Well, I changed my mind!" She had turned away, but glanced at him over her shoulder, her eyes still smoldering with heat and unfed passion. "Colin?"

He ran his fingers through his hair, knowing it was hopeless. They both looked as though they'd been well loved.

Loved.

Oh, no. "Yeah?" he asked warily.

"Sometimes people make mistakes, you know? Especially in marriage and affairs of the heart."

"Lani—"

"I know you were hurt the first time around, and

I'm so, so sorry. But for whatever reason, you're alone again." She touched him gently, slid her hand over his heart. "Maybe you could give love another try sometime...you know, with the right woman."

She thought he was still pining over his ex-wife. Nothing could be further from the truth, but how could someone like Lani understand? His wife had not only destroyed his belief in everlasting love, but she'd slept with his ex-partner as well, then had taken them both to the cleaners financially. He couldn't care less about the loss of that first fortune. Or even the marriage. But dammit, he still to this day mourned Max, with whom he'd been friends all his life.

He hadn't had a friend since, not a real one.

There had been no emotional attachments for him. He'd wanted nothing to worry about. Nothing to hurt over.

And now Lani was looking at him with those sweet, caring eyes, the ones that told him she was quickly becoming much more than a temporary situation in his life.

It scared him. It wasn't supposed to be like this.

"I would never hurt you, Colin," she whispered. "I'd be careful with your heart."

"Don't," he said hoarsely, rubbing a hand over his eyes. "I can't do this."

Something flickered in her expression. Hurt, and

even more devastating, disappointment. But she nodded and turned from him.

She reached for the lock, then hesitated, staring at the closed door for a long moment. "You'll have to try sometime, you know," she said softly to the wood. "You can't hide forever."

Watch me, he thought, hardening both his mind and his heart before he followed her out.

LANI CAME to Colin's house that night, her car loaded with ammunition.

Ammunition to make the house a home.

She had four more plants, two lovely watercolors painted by a local artist who was a casual friend of hers, and a framed picture of Colin she'd got from one of the recent newspaper articles written on him.

Her heart was armed, too, with compassion and patience. She hoped it would be enough.

Colin wasn't home. No surprise. Most likely he was still at his office, attempting to hide from what was happening between them.

She knew she was doing it again, pretending that this wasn't pretend. She could get seriously hurt that way and she knew it, but somehow she couldn't seem to help herself.

She couldn't explain it, this strange elation she felt, but for the first time in twenty-odd years, she was prepared to give her heart away. Hell, she was prepared to *toss* it away, hard and long, straight at Colin.

She couldn't wait until he was willing to catch it, but she didn't fool herself, she had lots of work ahead of her. Colin was no more ready to accept what was happening between them than she'd been only days before.

She had come to a rather startling realization. She wanted a real relationship. Not the superficial ones of her past, where she could, and did, walk away before any attachments occurred. She'd been doing that nearly all her life.

It was far too late to walk away from Colin.

How he would panic at her thoughts. He'd hate that she was thinking of a future beyond the pretense. What had happened in his marriage to make him so leery?

How could Lani convince him that it was okay to have loved and lost, but that he *had* to try again? Convince him that without love his heart would wither and die? That she knew this firsthand, and that together they could help one another?

While the house was quiet, she spread out the plants and the pictures, attacking the living room first. The other rooms would follow, gradually, and she could hardly imagine how wonderful the house would be when it was homey and warm.

But for now, she'd start with this room. It was crying out for attention. The floors were bare wood,

beautiful but...well, bare. The walls were a sophisticated, cool cream, and also far too stark. The brick
fireplace was empty, too, and she had just the picture
to hang over it.

Standing on a stepladder, she climbed high, hammer in hand. A dreamy smile crossed her face. It
would be so lovely in the winter, she thought, with a
fire blazing. Pretty pictures on the walls, some thick
rugs tossed here and there. She and Colin, together,
enjoying it.

Her dreamy smile grew into a full-fledged grin.
She couldn't wait.

Since the stepladder wasn't quite tall enough, she
got up on the very tippy top of it, where a bright or-
ange sticker warned her against doing that very
thing.

She stretched with all her might, the hammer precariously balanced in one hand, a nail in the other.
She was still grinning, ridiculously happy, anticipat-
ing the long, hot night ahead in Colin's arms.

"What the hell are you doing?"

At the unexpected, angry voice—Colin's voice—
Lani jerked.

And fell.

10

It all happened too fast. One moment Colin was staring at Lani and her hammer, the next she was far too still, in a terrifyingly crumpled heap on the floor.

Colin hit his knees on the stone hearth beside her, his hands cupping her face. "Lani!" *Oh, God, she didn't move.* "Lani!"

His heart was in his throat. She was lying too quietly. Quickly, he ran his hands over her body, but he didn't find anything broken.

Then he discovered the already huge bump on the back of her head, and let out one concise oath. "Lani? Come on, baby. Open your eyes."

She did, slowly, blinking in confusion and Colin took his first breath since he'd watched her tumble off the ladder.

"Don't get up," he demanded when she tried to sit. He held her down. "Don't move yet."

But she shifted, and at the movement her skin went green and pasty. "Nope, you're absolutely right," she said weakly, wincing. "No moving." And she closed her eyes.

Panic scampered up his spine. "Lani!"

"Shh." She groaned. "Please, don't...don't talk. My head is going to explode."

"Okay, that's it. Come on." As gently as he could, he scooped her into his arms.

Her head lolled against his chest and she moaned softly, lifting her hands to hold it still. "Put me down." Her voice was a thready murmur and Colin clenched his teeth at her obvious pain.

"We're going to the hospital. I think you have a concussion."

She blinked at him, clearly disoriented, and his alarm escalated.

"No hospital."

"You hit your head too damn hard on the stone hearth. We're going to get it checked out."

"No." But the protest was feeble, and her color was even worse now, her skin so light it was nearly transparent. "I'm...okay," she whispered. "Really."

Like hell. "Better safe than sorry. I want to make sure." He strode to the door, the warm, hurting bundle in his arms breaking his heart.

His fault, dammit.

"No doctor," she protested. "I told you...I'm fine."

"Let's prove it."

"Your mom and aunts...they think I'm cooking dinner while they're getting...manicures."

He could tell talking was difficult, and her words were slurred, making him walk even faster while trying to keep her cradled against him. "They can

fend for themselves." He had her in the foyer now
but the summer evening had chilled.

"They can't cook, Colin."

She was worried about his family when she
should be concentrating on herself. It wasn't a
stretch to express his fear for her in anger. "Look, if
they can learn to clean toilets, they can cook." Hoist-
ing her closer, he grabbed his denim jacket from the
closet with one hand and tried to toss it over her, but
she jerked in his arms.

"Down!"

"You're going to the hosp—"

"Colin—" She looked horrified and had gone pea-
green. "I'm not fine anymore."

He'd never felt like this—so full of fear over another human being. "I know, sweetheart, I'm just going to—"

"*Down*," she cried, shoving at him until he practically dropped her.

The hand she held frantically across her mouth finally clued him in and as she stumbled past him into
the kitchen, he went after her, wrapping a securing
arm around her waist as she leaned into the kitchen
sink and threw up.

"Go away," she told him halfway through, when
he was trying to hold back her hair and wipe her
forehead and support her all at the same time.

He didn't, but stayed right with her, fretting, pan-
icking, wondering if an ambulance would be faster.

When she was done, she sank to the floor and glared at him.

He braced himself for recriminations. He deserved it, whatever she said to him. He hunkered down beside her, the better to see into her hurting eyes.

"How could you call me sweetheart when I'm too sick to enjoy it?" she demanded, smacking him lightly on the chest.

He stared at her. "I did not call you that."

"Yes you did." She leaned against the cupboard and shivered. "I heard it."

"I— You're mistaken."

"No." Energy drained, she sighed wearily, a sound that pulled at some elementary core of him.

He pulled her close to him. "Any better at all?"

"Some." But she closed her eyes. Her body still shook, small tremors of shock that made *him* feel ill.

"How many fingers?" he pressed, holding up two.

"Too many." Miserable, she looked at the mess she'd made. "I just cleaned this kitchen."

Then, still in his arms, she fainted.

THE GOOD NEWS was that Lani's concussion wasn't serious.

The bad news was that they kept her overnight in the hospital.

Or maybe that was the good news in disguise, Colin thought grimly, as he showered the next morning. He'd spent a long, miserable night in a chair beside Lani's hospital bed watching her breathe.

Under different circumstances, she would have been in his arms, beneath him, writhing, sighing...coming.

Damn. He needed sleep.

It was really ironic, he decided, yanking a towel around his hips and studying his dark expression in the steamed mirror of his bathroom. Ironic that he hadn't been sure sleeping with Lani was the smart thing to do, and yet now that he'd decided differently, he couldn't manage to arrange it. He was getting a little tired of the constant erection he had going.

Like some lust-struck teen, he was mooning over a woman who had put her life on hold just to help him out. Her smile lit up his day and made him smile helplessly back. One affectionate touch from her could make his heart soar.

Truth was, he thought about her all the time when he was supposed to be concentrating on his project.

She made him laugh, made him think, made him want to please her, and in return he'd given her nothing but heartache and trouble.

He'd *yelled* at her, dammit. She'd been trying to warm up his house with her world, and he'd yelled at her.

She was going to be okay.

Gripping the edge of the sink, he bowed his head

and squeezed his eyes shut. She was going to be fine, she could come home this morning. The doctor had said so, both hers and the one he'd hired for a second opinion.

He closed his weary eyes, but then he had to relive in slow motion the sight of Lani falling, her huge eyes wide in terror, before her head cracked against the stone hearth.

In that first moment of horror for Colin, when she lay still, pale and unresponsive, he'd thought that if anything happened to her, he would die.

Then her eyes had flickered open.

He didn't want to go through anything like that ever again. Lani didn't remember the fall, but the doctor had assured them both that was normal.

Normal.

His Lani wasn't a normal woman, she was bright and sunny and almost painfully easy to love.

Love.

That had been his first, instinctive thought, and it was enough to have his blood pressure rocketing. He didn't love her, he *couldn't* love her. Couldn't love anyone.

He repeated this to himself as he raced through dressing. Then he broke three national speed records to get back to the hospital before Lani awoke and found herself alone.

But he didn't love her.

LANI WASN'T SLEEPING and she wasn't alone. She had both Lola and Bessie by her side telling her stories of Colin as a child.

They were wonderful, warm women, and hearing about Colin was heartwarming, but Lani could neither smile nor laugh. Her head throbbed. She was queasy, dizzy and tired.

And she wanted Colin.

Can't always have what you want, she told herself firmly, and forced her attention back to Colin's aunts. They were talking about the time Colin had taken apart the engine on his father's brand new BMW Sedan.

Colin had been twelve at the time.

She knew how smart he was and how precocious a child he must have been. She also knew how much his family loved him and wanted him to be happy.

Which was why, of course, they were doing their best to entertain her. She could tell they didn't quite understand what she saw in Colin, but they were grateful and relieved that she saw something. Since loyalty was everything to Lani, it endeared them to her.

"I'm going to be okay, you know," she told them. "You don't have to be here."

"Oh, honey. We *want* to be," Bessie said.

But both Bessie and Lola glanced for the hundredth time at the hospital door, and it made Lani smile even as tears burned her eyes. "I know what you're doing."

They tried to look innocent. "We're just watching over you," Lola said casually.

"You're afraid if you don't stay and guard things, namely me, that I'll leave Colin."

Their guilty faces said it all.

"I made a promise," she told them. "And to me, promises are sacred." They didn't have to know that the promise wasn't to love and cherish, but to lie.

Closing her eyes didn't shake the strange sense of melancholy, not when she kept reliving that moment just before her fall. The one she'd told Colin and the doctor she couldn't remember.

What the hell are you doing? Colin had demanded, the anger in his voice unmistakable.

She really was an idiot. A sentimental one, but an idiot all the same. How could she have thought he'd appreciate what she'd been trying to do to the house? *His* house.

Obviously he was so angry with her that he couldn't stand to see her. She'd been half out of it when he'd first brought her to the hospital and asleep by the time X rays had been finished. She'd slept fitfully all night in her darkened room, awakened every few hours by a nurse asking one silly question after another. She hadn't even bothered to open her eyes, but she hadn't heard Colin, not once.

It was morning now and still no sight of him.

Oh, yeah, she'd definitely blown it.

"The doctor said you're going to be fine enough to enjoy your engagement party," Bessie said now, quietly, "but if you don't think you'll be up to it, we'll understand."

They were so looking forward to it. And secretly, she had been, too. She may have had intimacy issues, but she was only human. A very female human at that. She had fantasies about her wedding, her real wedding, with a flowing white dress, a beautiful cake, an exotic honeymoon.

A huge, elaborate engagement party sounded so thrilling. If only it were real. "I'll be fine."

"Oh, good, because we're so excited. Look, I brought you something to read," Lola said, handing her a brightly colored bag. Lani pulled out a book with a red satin ribbon tied around it. *"How to Sexually Please a Man So That He'll Never Leave You?"*

Bessie gasped. *"Lola!* That's...that's pornography!"

"Not porn," Lola corrected with a dignified sniff. "Erotica." She exploded into giggles. "And it's very interesting reading, I'll have you know."

Lani flipped through the illustrations. "Wow!" They were graphic and definitely designed to titillate. She tipped her head to study a particularly interesting full-page photo. "Just...wow!"

Both sisters crowded close to see over her shoulder.

"Thought you might find something useful in there." Lola grinned. "Look at that. He's awfully good."

"Honestly, Lola." Bessie shook her head. "What's the sense in being a closet erotica reader if you're going to tell everyone?"

"Hey, I didn't tell her we read the book already." Lola blushed and bit her lip. "Oops."

Lani smiled around the pounding behind her eyes. "Thank you." She was surprised to find herself close to tears. "It means so much to me that you'd share."

"Oh, honey." Equally touched, Bessie smiled with suspiciously bright eyes.

Lola wasn't quite as sentimental, but she cared, too, and Lani knew it.

Lani fell asleep soon after, holding the book close to her heart.

WHEN COLIN came in a short time later, his aunts had been kicked out by the nurse. Lani was asleep, her expression tight from pain, her skin far too pale.

Fear stabbed him, even though her doctor had just signed her release. He whispered her name softly, not wanting to disturb her if she was sleeping deeply. She didn't budge. Gently, he touched her hand, the one holding a book close to her chest.

He took one look at the title and his eyes nearly bugged out of his head. "*How to Sexually Please a Man?*"

Lani's eyes flew open. "Colin!" She slipped the book under her blanket and tried to look casual.

"Interesting reading material."

She blushed wildly. "I don't know what you're talking about."

"Uh-huh." He tugged at her blanket until it came free. In her hands was the incriminating evidence.

Caught, she lifted her chin. "Your aunts gave it to me."

He started to laugh, then realized she was serious. "You're not kidding?"

"No."

He opened the book, and his eyes widened at some of the wilder illustrations. He pictured Lani reading it, getting ideas, and became aroused just at the thought. Slowly, he handed the book back to her.

Her eyes were shiny and aware and...hot. Very hot.

"You've read it," he said, his voice gravelly with the desire that never seemed to be far beneath the surface around her.

"A little," she admitted, dropping her gaze. "I wanted to know if it was true."

"If what was true?"

"If I sexually pleased you, would you never be able to leave? Or to ask *me* to?"

He stared at her. "I don't think you feel good enough for this conversation. You're pale and shaky. The doctor said—"

"Chicken."

"All right, fine." He didn't hedge, couldn't, not while pinned by the heat in her eyes. Rising from the uncomfortable chair where he'd spent the night, he sank to her bed, put a hand on either side of her hips. "I think you know that you sexually please me, Lani. In fact, we're so hot together, I'm surprised we haven't spontaneously combusted."

Her eyes smoldered.

He knew his did, too. "But I think you also know that what's happening to us is more than sex. Much more."

"And it's not what you wanted," she concluded, searching his face carefully.

"I never wanted such a connection, no," he admitted.

"I made you mad last night." Lani reached for one of his hands. "I was putting things in your house without asking, and now you don't want me anymore."

No. God, no. "I was mad at *me* last night, because when I walked in and saw what you were doing, and how right it all seemed, I panicked. I've been very busy, Lani, trying to avoid you and what you make me feel. My temper's frayed. All control is gone, flat gone." He studied her hand in his and sighed. "My project isn't getting done because I can't concentrate on work. That's never happened before. And when I look into your eyes, I see the terrifying truth."

"What truth?"

He grimaced, stood and walked the length of the hospital room before turning back to her.

Everything about her in the big white room seemed so vulnerable. Her pale features. Her narrow shoulders. Those expressive eyes.

"Colin, what truth?"

"I accused you of forgetting this was all pretend. But the truth is, it's me that keeps forgetting." He turned and stared grimly out the window.

Behind him, on the bed, Lani remained silent. "I'm sorry, I'm so damn sorry you got hurt," he said. "I sat there by you all night crucifying myself because it's my fault, but I can't go on like this. It has to be pretend between us, Lani. That's all it can be."

"You sat by me the entire night?"

He turned and saw the stunned surprise on her pale face. "Did you think I would leave you here alone?" But he saw that's exactly what she thought. He swore softly. "That's not very flattering."

"But it's just pretend between us." She repeated his words, slightly mocking. "What else would I think?"

"I care for you," he said carefully. "More than I want to. I've always been honest with you."

"Yes," she agreed, rubbing her head. "You're right. You've been honest. Don't worry, Colin, I don't blame you. There's no reason for all that guilt I see on your face."

"You're free to leave here," he said quietly, coming close. "But you need rest and to be taken care of. Will you let me bring you home?"

"Are you worried I'll renege on our deal?"

"No," he lied.

Lani let out a little laugh, which made her wince. She tossed back her covers and stood shakily, pushing his hand away when he tried to help steady her. "I'm fine, I don't need taking care of. Just a little headache, that's all." Her eyes were unusually cool, even as she weaved a bit on her feet. "And yes, I'll come with you. I gave you my word, remember?"

He remembered. And hated himself for it.

"HOW LONG are you going to be mad at me?" Colin asked.

Lani was sprawled in his bed. He couldn't help but notice she was wearing a T-shirt, *his* T-shirt, and she looked so damn good he had to stay at the door so that he could be sure to control himself.

She didn't answer him.

Her face was pale. Her eyes were lined with delicate purple shadows. His heart hurt just looking at her. "Lani?"

She leaned back against his pillows, her face inscrutable. "I'm going to be mad for a while. Probably." She looked away. "Well, for at least a few more minutes."

"Isn't there anything I can do to change that?"

"Sure." She met his gaze again, her eyes daring him. "Tell me about the ex-wife you still love."

"Lani."

"That's what I thought. Too chicken."

How was he supposed to tell her that he wasn't nursing that kind of pain, but a deeper one, the betrayal and loss of his best friend? It humiliated him, shamed him. "I'd rather talk about that fascinating book." He gestured to the erotica sitting on his nightstand. It was open, and when he moved closer he saw the chapter she'd been reading was titled, "Pleasure Him Every Night and You'll Never Regret It. Here's How."

"Did you finish that chapter?" he asked, his voice thick.

"Maybe." Her lips quirked, and in that moment, he saw a flicker of the warm, loving Lani he'd come to care for so much.

Unable to stop himself, he smiled at her. "That looks good, that almost-smile on your face. I missed that."

"Oh, Colin." She melted, all ice gone. "You drive me crazy, but I miss you."

"I'm right here."

"That's not what I meant."

He knew what she meant, and he was helpless against the pull of the promise in her voice. But there was lingering hurt there, too, hurt *he'd* put there.

She was willing to listen to his past. His hurts. And

suddenly, he wanted to tell her everything. "I don't still love my ex-wife. And I'm not pining away for her, either. It's not what you think."

"Then tell me."

"It was a long time ago. I thought we were happy, even though I knew she'd married me for my money—"

"Oh, Colin."

"It's true, and it's okay," he told her, hating the pity, knowing there'd be more before he was through. "I wanted her, too. She was beautiful and elegant and everything I thought I'd need. We were young, just out of school." He lifted a shoulder. "I worked a lot, and she hated that. She needed attention, lots of it, and I didn't give it. I couldn't—the truth is, I didn't see what the problem was. So, out of boredom, she struck up a friendship with my partner, my best friend, Max. She started off trying to convince him to have me work less. She ended up convincing him to—" Unable to stand still, he walked the length of his bedroom to stare out the picture window. "You know, I've never said any of this out loud. I've never been able to tell anyone."

"You can tell me," said Lani quietly from the bed. "You can tell me anything."

"I know." He drew in a deep breath and concentrated on the garden beyond his window. "She seduced Max, stole all my money and left town. Six months later I received divorce papers in the mail."

"How long ago was this?" she asked gently.

"Five years. I guess you could say I've not let a lot of people close to me since then."

"I think that's a fair assessment."

There was so much compassion in her voice he couldn't look at her. "I still blame her for Max," he said roughly. "We'd been friends all my life." He tried to be distant and tough, willing Lani to understand, to somehow help him resist her. "I promised myself I'd never get involved again. *Ever.* And I meant it."

"You're blaming the wrong person," she said quietly.

"I'm not blaming you."

"I meant yourself. It wasn't your fault. And it wasn't all hers, either. Your friend betrayed you, too, not just your wife. You were hit twice, hard, and I don't blame you for remaining hurt all this time. But Colin, not all women are so weak. Not all of us will betray their vows, and break the law while they're at it."

He shook his head. "I don't blame all women. That would be silly."

"Very," Lani agreed. "But I just realized, I haven't been as patient as I could be. I'll try harder, and maybe you will, too." Scooting to one side of the bed, she lifted his own covers, wordlessly inviting him in. "We're in a situation neither of us are easy with, but

I think we can still salvage something and make the most of it, don't you?"

His heart was suddenly in his throat.

"Won't you hold me?" she asked. "Hold me as we've both wanted for too long now?"

He was there, doing exactly that, with no recollection of kicking off his shoes and diving into the bed.

With a slow touch, she smoothed his hair back and ran her fingers over his face. She cupped his jaw, studying him.

"What do you see?"

"You." She smiled. "There's not much of the successful inventor here right now." She looked pleased at that, and laughed when he frowned. "Don't get me wrong," she assured him. "I like that man. But this one—" her thumb slid over his lower lip and his entire body tightened in response "—this man is so much more. He's warm and loving and incredibly handsome. Colin..." her voice went husky with emotion "...you're the most wonderful thing in my life."

He knew he was staring at her with a dopey look of wonder on his face, and for once he couldn't master the control to mask it. She looped her arms around his neck and kissed him softly, then less softly. Then with her tongue.

"Must have been a hell of a chapter," he said, gasping when they broke apart for air.

She let out a slow, sexy grin that had him grinning back in return. "Yeah, it was." She snuggled close, pressing all those warm, lush curves against him. "Want to know what I learned?"

Before he could answer, she had snaked her hands beneath his shirt, touching him with eager, seeking hands. She unbuttoned his shirt, then shoved it off so she could touch his chest. Not stopping there, she slid the zipper on his pants down, then looked up at him. "If anyone stops us this time, I'm going to hurt them."

He let out a laugh that ended up as a groan because she'd slipped her hands inside and touched everything she found, and she'd found plenty.

Desire pumped through him as he buried all ten fingers in her cloud of blond hair, and holding her to him, seared them both with a long soul-searching kiss. It surprised him, this desperate need he had to keep that connection, that special, hot, wet mating of tongues. "Was this in the book?" he asked.

"No, I made all that up. Here—" She laughed breathlessly as she cupped him in her palms. Her fingers moved on him and he nearly lost it. "*That's* in the book," she whispered, breathing heavily in his ear. "And so is this..."

He moaned under her greedy fingers.

He wanted her skin to skin, wanted her legs entwined with his, wanted, wanted, wanted *everything*. It had been so long for him, and with all their aborted attempts at lovemaking over the past days, he was painfully aroused, so much so that his bones ached with it. "I want to see you," he murmured, and pulled off her shirt.

She wasn't wearing anything underneath.

Enthralled, he watched his fingers on her pale breasts, mesmerized by the way her nipples hardened when he tormented them with the tip of his tongue. He untied her sweatpants and slowly slid them down her smooth, toned legs.

She wasn't wearing anything beneath them, either, and he groaned at the sight stretched out before him. "Oh, baby," he whispered. "You're something. I've got to taste you."

She gripped and ungripped fistfuls of the sheets, writhing beneath him, panting his name as he traced over her with his tongue. When she shattered, crying and shuddering, he held her, rocked her as she slowly came back to her senses. Then he started all over again.

"I want you..." she managed when she could "...inside me."

He couldn't breathe, couldn't think beyond doing just that. He reached into his drawer by the bed, into the box he'd put there and tore open a foil packet while she watched, her eyes heavy and full of promise.

He came back to her, letting out a shuddery breath at the feel of her beneath him. "Open for me," he whispered. "Yeah..." he moaned as he sank in deep "...just like that."

She sighed his name.

"Wrap your legs.... Ahh, Lani." He buried his face in the softness of her neck, surrounding himself with her. He could never get enough, never. He felt her muscles start to shake as he slowly pulled back, then again sank into her.

Her head tossed back and forth on the pillow.

He thrust again. And then again. Because he had to, he gathered her close and watched as her eyes glazed, as she gripped him tight and sobbed his name.

His last conscious thought before he followed her into paradise was that if she read the rest of that book, she just might kill him.

11

HE OVERSLEPT. A shock, because Colin never over-slept. His inner clock was as reliable as any alarm...or had been until this morning.

He was sprawled on his stomach, and given the chill hitting his bare butt, the covers were long gone. Groggy, he lifted his head and groaned when he saw that it was nearly nine o'clock.

His staff would get a big kick out of this since he knew Claudia had made certain each and every one knew about his engagement.

He'd get those sly looks, the ones that said they knew *exactly* what he'd been doing all night long.

They'd be right. He cracked open another eye and saw the empty foil packets scattered on the floor. He grinned. Oh, yeah, they'd made a considerable dent in his supply.

He felt insatiable. Unable to stop grinning, he rolled over, ready for more.

But he was alone.

Lani was gone. There was an indentation on the pillow where her head had been, giving him hazy images of how they'd finally slept, limbs entangled, faces close, but the sheets were cold now.

His heart constricted. No reason for panic, he told himself. It had just been sex.

Really *great* sex.

Then he saw the note on the nightstand.

Colin,
Had to work. Couldn't bring myself to wake you, you looked too cute.
Looking forward to sharing the next chapter in the book.

Love, Lani

Cute? He wasn't cute. But just thinking about the next chapter brought his early morning hard-on to new levels of *hard*.

He hit the shower, closed his eyes to the hot, pounding spray and pretended that the "Love, Lani" part of the note didn't mean what he knew it did.

He had nearly convinced himself it was nothing, just a way of signing a note, when he walked into his kitchen. He was still barefoot, his shirt unbuttoned, a tie hanging loose around his neck in anticipation of a meeting with the Institute's founder.

Had Lani eaten? he wondered.

The thought stopped him in his tracks. He wasn't her keeper. She'd been managing to take care of herself for some time now without any help at all. He shouldn't worry.

But this strange protective possessiveness was startling and not a little uncomfortable. "It'll pass," he assured himself, coming to an abrupt stop.

Sitting at his table were his mother, Bessie and Lola, wearing wide, knowing grins.

"What?" he grumbled. "You've never seen a man desperate for coffee before?"

"Is that all you're desperate for?" Lola asked sweetly.

"In my books, a man's in bad shape when he talks to himself," Bessie decided. "And can't even properly dress himself for company." She tsked at his appearance.

Scowling, Colin started to button his shirt. "Since when are you company?"

"Darling." His mother looked at him with tenderness. "You seem a bit...well, unlike yourself."

"I'm late." He moved to the counter.

"We're here because we love you, you know that."

"I thought you were here to torture me." The last button at his neck felt like a noose.

"No, that was before you got engaged. The point is, we're here for you." His mother was hedging a bit, which was very unlike her. "By any chance," she asked, "Is there anything—anything at all—that you'd like to talk to us about?"

He laughed. "I know all about the birds and the bees, Mother, thanks."

"Oh, you." But she laughed, too. "You know what I mean."

He thought about thanking his aunt Bessie for giving Lani such delightful reading material. Thought also about thanking them for the previous interruptions because last night had been the most incredibly passionate night of his life.

"I'm fine," he said instead.

"And in love," Lola added.

Whoa. All three women were watching him now, waiting breathlessly on the edges of their seats.

"Right?" Bessie pressed. "You're totally, one-hundred-percent, can't-live-without-her, irrevocably, head-over-heels in love?"

He shook his head. "Okay, what's this really about?"

"We saw Lani this morning," his mother said. "She practically floated down the stairs. She's lovely, Son, and so special. I love her already."

"But?"

"But if you're just toying with her to get me off your back, I'll never forgive myself."

"Frankly, Colin," Bessie interrupted, "we're not sure you deserve her."

"*What?*" He couldn't believe it. "You've been hounding me to get married, and now—"

"If you hurt that dear, sweet child..."

"Believe me, she's not a child," he informed his mother.

"Colin!" Lola gave him the evil eye. "Don't forget, we brought you into this world, and trust me, we can take you out again."

Colin managed to laugh. "This is a joke."

His mother stood and came close. She reached for his hands, touching him for the first time in a long time. "Colin, I love you. I want you to be happy. I think you could have that with Lani, but I don't know if you're going to let yourself do it. If you don't, or can't, you're going to hurt her. I feel responsible for that."

"Well, don't."

Her smile was sad. "I can't help it. Let go, Colin. Let go of your painful past and move on. That's all I want for you. I'd like to see you let yourself love with Lani."

"How do you know I'm not?"

"I know."

"I don't have time for this," he decided, pulling away. He grabbed his keys from the counter. "I wish the three of you would make up your damn minds. You want me married, you don't want me married...you're driving me crazy. I have work."

But it wasn't work he thought about on the drive into town; it was a sweet, blue-eyed blonde.

COLIN PARKED and entered his building. Just being here made him feel better.

Today he'd be able to work. *Had* to work. He had some great ideas he wanted to start on right away.

Claudia stood when he came to her desk. Her face was pale and she looked as if she had a terrible secret.

His stomach fell. "What's up?"

"Here's your messages." She handed him a small stack of notes.

"Claudia, what's the matter?"

"Maybe you should get some coffee before you head to your office?"

"No, I need to get started. Are you all right?"

Again she dodged the question. "Your cleaning crew is still in there."

Lani. His heart leaped. "Okay."

"Um..." She hesitated, then shook her head. "Never mind."

With one last look at her, Colin walked down the hallway, thinking Lani shouldn't be working, not so soon after her concussion. She should be in bed. Maybe he'd put her there himself.

Yeah, he liked that idea.

Then he stood in the doorway to his office, staring in horror at the crushed mess of metal and delicate laser model laying on his floor. Above it, tears in her eyes, stood Lani.

Carmen stood quietly next to her, looking both defeated and afraid. Refusing to acknowledge Colin's presence, she stared at her clenched hands.

He gritted his teeth. His ruined prototype looked like a cheap two-dollar toy.

"I'm so sorry, Colin," Lani said quickly. "It was a terrible accident. Carmen was dusting and—"

"It's ruined."

His eyes were dark, angry and colder than Lani had ever seen them. "Yes, I know. I'm so sorry."

"I'd like to talk to you alone," he said in a terribly quiet voice.

"But—"

"Now."

Lani could hardly move she was so upset. Awkwardly, she made a few signs, and for once Carmen didn't pretend to not understand.

With one last furtive glance at Colin, the older woman escaped through the door.

It was the first time she'd left Colin's presence without sticking out her tongue.

Despite Lani's best efforts not to cry, two tears squeezed out, slid down her cheeks. "God, Colin. I feel sick."

"That's because you shouldn't be working today, dammit."

"Not from the concussion. From what I've done! Tell me the cost of the damage."

"It's irreplaceable, Lani."

It was his tone that got her, that distant tone that told her she was nothing to him but an irresponsible maid. "Everything can be replaced for the right amount," she said. "Tell me the cost and I promise to somehow—"

He laughed. *Laughed.* "You could work for the rest of your life cleaning and still not make enough."

The implication of that sank in. She knew he was angry, he had a right to be. She had made a horrible, heart-breaking mistake and she would do anything she could to rectify it.

What couldn't be rectified was her pride. "Are you telling me there's nothing I can do to make this better?"

"Firing her would be a great start."

"Carmen?"

"Who else?"

"I..." She didn't understand why he would ask such a thing, but she thought of Carmen's three grandchildren, the ones that Carmen struggled to raise by herself. Lani could never live with herself if she fired the woman, but that was beside the point. She would never choose the welfare of four lives over the value of one thing, no matter how important that one thing was. "I can't believe you can ask me to do that."

"I'm not asking, I'm telling."

"I don't follow orders well," she warned him, her voice shaking. "Not even for you."

"You'd keep her after this?" he asked incredulously. "After she broke the laser prototype?"

Now she understood and was overwhelmed with

sadness for his quick judgment. "Carmen didn't break the model, Colin. *I* did."

"No."

"I tried to tell you, you didn't want to listen. Carmen was dusting and saw a spider. She made a funny strangled noise and I jerked around. When I did, my elbow bumped the laser. It shattered before I could catch it."

His eyes were hard and shuttered. "You're covering for her. You wouldn't be so clumsy."

The sorrow spread through her veins, killing her spirit. "Then you don't know very much about me. Certainly less than I thought if you think I'd fire Carmen over my own error."

"I know you better than you think. You have a save-the-world-heart. You're trying to save Carmen, and she doesn't deserve it."

"I'm telling you, it wasn't her fault."

He stared at her, clearly unable to believe she could be so loyal. But then again, he hadn't had a lot of loyalty in his life. She tried to remember this and looked for a sign of the warm, loving, passionate man she'd been with the night before.

He was completely gone, hidden behind a mask of grim, unforgiving anger.

But she did see a flicker of something that looked suspiciously like fear, and it made her heart hurt. "You're using this as an excuse to push me away," she realized. "Did last night scare you that much?"

A tightening of his lips was her only answer.

"It was the real thing and you can't take it." She let out a hurt little laugh. "I'm right, aren't I? You can't trust me enough to give me your heart. You woke up and panicked. You needed a reason to be hard and ungiving, to back off and tell yourself you were right in doing so. I just gave you that excuse. Well, damn you, Colin West. After all we've shared, you still can't do it. You can't let yourself love me."

"You're forgetting again, dammit, that this is all pretend."

"Oh, no. It stopped being pretend the moment you first touched me, and you know it. And even if you somehow didn't, then last night should have proved it to you once and for all."

"No." But his voice was hoarse. "You agreed to this, Lani. I knew I was asking a lot, but you agreed to play house. It's all a show."

He was right, but that only made her feel worse. She wrapped her arms around herself for comfort. "I realize this is the last straw for you, Colin. You see your project set back even further now. You see me having to stay longer. You see your peaceful, quiet existence permanently in your past. I understand. I'll back out of this office job. And out of the deal, if you'd like. But don't you dare lie to my face and tell me you never had feelings for me."

He dragged in a ragged breath and admitted nothing.

She looked at him, hoping to find a piece of the man she'd fallen for, but there was no one but the successful, rich, disdainful inventor, the one who could and would trust no one.

"I was there last night," she said urgently, trying one last time to reach him, knowing this was her last chance. "I saw your face when we made love, I saw the wonder and the affection and the heat swimming in your eyes. You can't tell me it was fake. I won't believe you."

Colin had no idea what to say to her, not when his head was spinning with the need to run away, far and fast. Yes, he lusted after her, deeply. But lust wasn't love.

He didn't do love.

He simply couldn't allow himself to fall for this woman who had turned his life upside down without trying. Couldn't allow himself to get in that deep because he wouldn't be able to take it when it was over.

"Obviously you're not ready for this," she said, pinching her lips together. He thought he saw more moisture fill her eyes, which was like a knife to his gut, but she blinked, clearing it away.

Gently, she scooped the shattered laser onto her dustpan, then very carefully set the entire mess on his desk. "I'm very sorry, Colin," she said quietly, straightening. "I'd do anything to be able to take it back. I know I can't. I only wish that you'd understand I'd rather rip out my own heart than hurt you."

He didn't say a word when she came close, smelling like sweet summer rain, looking strong yet vulnerable in a way that made him want to throw everything he'd said out the window. With an incredibly light touch, she set her hands on his shoulders, bracing herself so that she could reach up on tiptoe to kiss his cheek.

"Good-bye," she whispered.

Then she was gone.

Colin stood there, still frozen. He had been blown away by her intense determination to break through to him, by her fierce loyalty to Carmen, by her need to make him understand. That she had walked away now, when he knew damn well how much his business meant to her own, caused a deep, piercing ache.

He was an idiot. A big, dumb jerk. He was taking his frustrations out on her and an old woman for God's sake.

For an encore he'd have to go beat up some orphans.

Disgusted with himself, he walked to his desk and took a good long look at what he'd put before everything else. Pieces of metal, nothing more.

Shattered, like his heart.

He looked at the closed door, certain he'd just let the best thing ever to happen to him get away.

IT WAS PAST MIDNIGHT before he allowed himself to go home. He was heavy-footed and bleary-eyed.

And just maybe exhausted enough to crawl into bed without missing Lani.

The house was dark, a good thing because no way could he face his mother and aunts and admit his failure. Or that the engagement party, scheduled for tomorrow night, was pretty much a moot point.

He turned his shower on boiling hot and stood under it for a long time, but the tension inside him didn't drain away. Naked and wet, he padded out of the bathroom into his dark room, hoping to fall into the oblivion of sleep.

"Hey."

It was the sweetest, softest, sexiest "hey" he'd ever heard, and it had come from the vicinity of his bed.

"Hey back," he said, so ridiculously relieved that his voice sounded like gravel. He peered into the moonlit dark and saw the shadow of Lani sitting cross-legged on his bed.

"I thought you'd never get out of that shower."

Her voice held a touching mix of affection and nerves. He'd never been so happy to see anyone in his life, even though he couldn't exactly *see* her. He came closer to make sure he wasn't dreaming. His knees touched the bed. "I thought you were gone."

"You fired me from the cleaning job," she said slowly, touching his arm when he reached for the lamp. "Not yet, Colin. I'll say this better in the dark."

She drew in a ragged breath. "You didn't say anything about this, about our agreement, so I didn't
know, but...I didn't want to go back on my word. I
still want to help you, if you want me."

He didn't deserve her.

"I'm so sorry, Colin," she said quickly before he
could say a word. "I'm so, so sorry about your work,
about what I did to the laser. Please forgive me."

God. He'd yelled at her, been a complete jerk and
she was apologizing to him. He was slime.

Worse.

And completely incapable of keeping his distance,
not tonight. Hell, he couldn't even remember why
he'd ever wanted to.

"Colin?" She was still worried, still half braced for
his rejection.

He had to see her. He overrode her hand on his
arm and flipped on the light, thinking only that he
had to look into her gorgeous eyes.

Her startled gasp filled the room and he remembered...he was totally nude.

"Colin..." Her eyes feasted on him, feeding the
heat and hunger that were already nearly out of control. "You're so beautiful," she said dreamily.

"Not like you." His gaze never left her face. She
could have been wearing a potato sack for all he
cared. "Not like you, Lani. You're the most beautiful
sight I've ever seen." Slowly he lowered himself to

the bed, then dragged her close. Banding his arms around her, he bent his head to hers.

"Does this mean you forgive me...?"

"Don't," he begged. "Don't ever apologize to me for today. I can't believe how I talked to you, how you looked when I did. I know that you've lost too many people in your life—"

She went utterly still.

He cupped her face, made her look at him when she would have pulled away. "You never told me about it. About your family."

"I...couldn't. It was a long time ago, it doesn't matter now."

"It still gives you nightmares, it matters. I'm so sorry, Lani. I will never forgive myself for how I treated you."

"I will," she said simply.

Unable to bear hearing the words that came straight from her heart, when his own was so over-flowing and confused, he kissed her. Blind, obsessive heat consumed them but it was different this time, different from anything he'd ever known.

It was soul-searching, earth-shattering and incredibly tender. The urgency was there, but suddenly they had all the time in the world, at least all night, and knowing that, Colin was hopelessly caught by every little nuance, the whisper of a kiss, the slightest touch, a promising glance.

It started again before it was over, the passion, the

hunger, and while the initial desperation was gone, the need remained.

He needed her, and he knew without a doubt that she needed him, too.

Nothing in his life had ever felt so...right. So perfect, though even that word didn't do justice to what they shared in those magical hours between midnight and dawn.

"I love you, Colin," Lani whispered at one point, the pale moonlight highlighting her lovely features. "I'll love you forever." Then she kissed him, halting any words or panic, and for the rest of the long, dark night, he lost himself in her.

12

THE NEXT DAY Lani literally danced down Colin's hallways.

It wasn't pretend anymore between Colin and her, it couldn't be. Not with all they'd shared the night before.

Deliriously happy, she danced right to work, starting with Colin's house. She had lots to do—too much, given how behind she'd gotten yesterday, but she didn't mind.

Work was great. Life was great.

She was great.

And tonight—her engagement party.

Hugging herself, she grinned with excitement. Then got to work, starting with the downstairs. She was in the room next to Colin's office, very carefully dusting the bookshelves, concentrating intensely. The last thing she wanted to do was break something else.

In the next room, she heard Colin's office phone, heard his rich, deep voice answer and greet Claudia.

Lani tried to ignore what the mere sound of him

did to her. She sprayed furniture polish on her cloth and turned her attention to the shelf.

Through the wall came the low, sexy timbre of Colin's voice. She didn't listen to the words, that would be eavesdropping, and Lani respected his privacy too much for that.

But she wasn't above losing herself in the simple sound of him. She'd done the same last night, listening to his husky whispers as he'd made love to her. Just the thought of some of those wicked suggestions brought a heat to her face now. For a dark, driven man, Colin was earthy, uninhibited and amazingly sensual.

She loved it.

Then she heard the word *wedding* from the other side of the wall and she stilled.

Wedding? He was talking to Claudia about a wedding? It was wrong to listen, she knew that, but she couldn't tear herself away.

"I realize you just want to help," he was saying. "But it's not necessary."

Lani put a hand to the wall to steady herself. There was going to be a wedding? *Theirs?*

"No, Claudia. You don't understand." He spoke more quietly now, so that Lani had to strain to hear. And strain she did, plastering her ear to the wall.

"It's not necessary," Colin said. "Because there isn't going to be a wedding."

The rag and polish can fell from Lani's hands to

the thick carpet as her raging emotions went from a sudden high to an all-time low.

It's all right, she told herself, scooping up her supplies. They'd not discussed anything yet. There was plenty of time.

And she should walk away now, before she heard something she shouldn't.

"I didn't want to tell you about it for this very reason," came Colin's voice. "I knew you'd react this way— No, listen to me, Claudia. I'm not trying to shut you out of being involved. It's not like that at all. My engagement to Lani? It's not real. It never was."

His voice was so calm and certain. So mundane, as if he were discussing dinner plans.

Lani staggered away from the wall. *Shouldn't have listened*, she chastised herself, but it was too late. Her heart was processing the words her brain had heard, and it hurt. God, it hurt.

Colin made a disparaging sound. "Yes, that's right. It was all a sham, designed to let me work. There's not going to be a wedding. Ever." His certainty was unmistakable.

Lani's heart broke.

Colin had never dropped the pretense. The realization wasn't an easy one. Last night—oh, last night—she covered her hot face. She'd been so free with herself, so into the beauty of what they'd shared, and it hadn't been real.

She should have known. After all, he'd been careful to make her no promises. She had no one to blame for the anguish she felt now, no one but herself.

Facing the truth was a humiliating experience, and far more painful than she could have believed. No matter what she had told herself, no matter what she'd thought she'd seen in Colin's eyes, she had been the only one to fall.

Lani just barely managed to scoop up her bucket and get out of the room without falling apart. Her vision hampered by bright, hot tears, her throat clogged with stinging hurt, her head down so that she could concentrate on getting her feet to cooperate, she escaped.

And ran directly into Irene in the hallway.

"Darling?" Irene frowned with worry.

Lani's heart was at her feet, crushed, and she was seconds away from self-destructing. Irene's sympathetic smile nearly killed her.

"Are you all right? What's the matter?" Irene wanted to know.

What was the matter? Her heart was broken. She wanted the man of her dreams to fall in love with her. She wanted him to need her above all else. She wanted, oh, how she wanted, to be a *real* bride. For Colin.

"Lani?"

"Nothing," she answered quickly, her chest hitching with pain. "It's nothing." She let out a little laugh to mask her quiet sob. "I just got a dust fleck in my eye, that's all. Excuse me—"

But Irene gently took her arms and held her still. "You don't have to hide from me. I can see what's happened plain as the nose on my face."

"I doubt it."

"My son hurt you."

"Oh, no. He would never—"

"Not physically," Irene agreed. "Of course not. But he hurt you all the same. No need to rush to the rat's defense."

Lani cleared her throat and swallowed her tears, hoping she sounded normal. "He's a wonderful man, smart and—"

"Lani—"

"—and responsible and strong and—" Her voice cracked when Irene's sad smile threatened her control.

"Oh, Lani. I know what Colin's good points are. Believe me, I know. But I also know the man's faults, and one of them is an inability to open his heart to another."

The tears Lani had been holding back betrayed her and several spilled over. "It's not his fault," she whispered. "He's been hurt." She sniffed and wiped her face. "He's afraid."

"And now you're paying the price." Irene made a small noise of distress. "I shouldn't have pushed him into this. I'm so sorry."

More than anything in that moment, Lani needed love, desperately. She needed a hug, needed to feel the warmth. It seemed natural to surge forward and hug Irene tight.

It took Irene only one second of hesitation before she wrapped her arms around Lani. "I'm sorry. So, so sorry," she murmured, her voice rough with her own unshed tears.

The affection from a woman very unused to such things made Lani cry harder, but it was worth it. For one last special moment, she held onto a part of Colin's life. A life she'd wanted for herself with all her heart. "I have to go," she whispered, knowing if she hung around now she'd make a fool of herself.

Irene straightened away, her own eyes suspiciously damp. "Where? What will happen?"

"I don't know."

Irene's gaze was still hurting, but searching, too. "Truth, Lani. Was this engagement ever real?"

Only for herself. It'd been all too real. And short.

"Damn him," Irene breathed when Lani didn't answer. "How could he have done this to you? To me? To the entire town? It's unthinkable."

"Don't judge him too harshly," Lani begged. "He had his reasons and they were unselfish ones. He didn't want to hurt you or anyone else."

Irene nodded, looking thoughtful. "Yes, I see where he thought he was doing the right thing. Maybe there's hope for him then."

Lani couldn't imagine it; she'd given him everything she'd had and that hadn't been good enough.
She had nothing left but her pride, and she was taking that home. "I'm sorry about tonight." The
thought of her engagement party seemed...obscene.
"Will you be all right?"

"Don't you dare worry about me." For the first
time since they'd met, Irene made the first move of
physical affection. She reached out and clasped
Lani's hands. "Are you sure you have to leave?
There's nothing left?"

There was plenty left. Too much. It was why she
had to go. "I have to leave, Irene. For me. Do you understand?"

"I don't want to, but of course I do. Lani, darling..." her eyes filled again "...take care."

And so, for the second time in her life, Lani lost a
mother. She wanted to hate Colin for that alone, but
couldn't. Not when she understood him so well.

She managed to walk away, but it was the hardest
thing she'd ever done. Remembering his last words
helped.

It's not real, he'd said. *It never was.*

By leaving, she was breaking her word to Colin,
something she'd sworn never to do, but it could no
longer be helped.

It took her a pathetically short amount of time to
pack—less than three minutes. She left the cool
house and stepped out into the simmering heat. She

got in her car, rolled down her windows and drove off while Colin was still in his office, probably still on his phone casually denying everything she had believed in.

Risk.

She'd wanted one, and in the bargain had gotten far more than she'd counted on. Oh, well, it was done. She wouldn't regret it.

She headed down the hill and crossed the tracks.

COLIN HEARD the front door shut. Between himself and Lani, and now his family, he heard the sound many times a day.

But for some reason, this time his head came up. His heart clenched. A very bad feeling filled his gut.

Something was wrong.

Claudia was still talking in his ear so he shook off the feeling and made a new attempt to listen to her listing his messages. They were important, he knew this, but he couldn't concentrate.

Not when inside him there was a sudden, terrifying aloneness. "I'm sorry, Claudia, I've got to go." He hung up the phone, then went still as he tried to place his sudden uneasiness.

The house was silent as it hadn't been since...since before Lani had come into his life. He got up and left the office.

The living room was empty. So was the kitchen. His unease grew. "Lani?" he called out.

Nothing. No sweet voice, no musical, contagious laughter.

Spurred on by a strange fear, he raced up the stairs. She wasn't in the bedroom, where he'd left her soundly sleeping only a little while before. He remembered how she'd looked when he came out of the shower, sleeping so peacefully, looking heart-wrenchingly at home in his huge bed, wearing nothing more than his sheets and a contented expression.

Now she was gone.

Probably at work, he assured himself.

But the panic persisted. He looked in the bathroom.

Her toothbrush was gone.

So was her hairbrush and her small bag of makeup. Heart racing, palms damp, Colin raced back into the bedroom, but there was no mistake.

All her clothes were gone.

She'd left him.

She'd broken her promise and—

"Well, Son, you finally did it," said his mother from behind him. "Chased away the best thing ever to happen to you."

"She's...gone," he said, stunned. His thoughts raced back to last night, to their incredible night of passion. Had she been upset, even as he'd held her, touched her, tasted her? Remembering her soft cries, her not-so-soft demands for more, the way she'd held him clenched tight to her, he knew she hadn't been holding back, harboring any resentment.

She was too honest for that.

But was he honest enough to see the truth? He knew she loved him, knew that he hadn't been able to say those words back to her.

And he knew, dammit, he knew that eventually what he'd given her wouldn't be enough. She'd want the pretense dropped once and for all.

She'd want him for real.

Why hadn't he given her that? Why had he held on to his fear in the face of the most incredulous, giving love he'd ever received? "She's really gone," he said again, bewildered, sinking to his bed. He looked around him as if she might materialize out of nowhere. "Gone."

"Yes," his mother said.

"She promised." He had no idea why he said it, it just popped out, and he wouldn't take back the words because suddenly pride meant nothing. "She *promised.*"

"Promised what?"

No, dammit. He couldn't pin this on her. This was his fault, all his fault. "What happened?"

"She came out of the room next to your office, looking like she'd seen a ghost..." She paused. "Or maybe she heard something? Something that would hurt her?"

Colin closed his eyes, knowing what he'd done.

What she'd heard, and how it would have crushed her.

Claudia had been so eager to help, so eager to rush him down the aisle, and he'd balked.

But even as he'd done so, he'd known in his heart he wanted to throw the deception out the window and hold Lani to him forever. *Forever.* And that meant vows.

So why had he been so adamant with Claudia? Stubbornness, pure and simple, and Lani had been on the other side of the wall, unable to see the truth in his eyes, hearing only what he had said to his secretary.

It's not real, it never was.

He'd said that to Claudia and Lani had heard him and believed it. Why wouldn't she? He'd certainly said it enough.

Just another lie.

He swore.

"Oh, yes, it's a mess," his mother agreed solemnly. "And you only realize the half of it."

"What are you talking about?"

"In less than eight hours everyone that knows you is converging here for the engagement party of the year. It's going to be unpleasant without a fiancée, Colin."

"That's the least of my problems at the moment." He sighed and looked into his mother's hurt eyes. "I'm sorry."

"I don't think I'm the one you should be apologizing to."

"No, you're wrong about that. I tried to fool you. I lied to you."

His mother gave him a sad, forgiving smile. "I might still have been furious, but Lani pointed out that you had good reasons and even better intentions, and I have to agree with her." She sat next to him. "You're a wonderful man, Colin. You can run your own life perfectly well and I shouldn't have tried to interfere. I hope you'll forgive me for that."

She startled them both by giving him a fiercely loving hug. "You'll do what's right now," she whispered, squeezing him close. "I have faith in you."

Then she left him alone.

It was the emptiness that scared Colin the most, the deep, ripping loneliness already filling his heart. That he had caused Lani to feel the same way was unforgivable. She deserved so much more.

He wanted to give it to her, if only she'd let him.

Having no idea how he was going to make this all better, only knowing he had to try, he went after her.

SEVERAL HOURS LATER, in the thick, repressive heat, Colin had to admit failure.

Lani had vanished.

She wasn't at her office, wasn't on a job, wasn't in her apartment.

He'd got a fulminating look from Great-Aunt Jennie, one that should have withered him on the spot, but he was already so miserable she couldn't possibly make him feel worse.

He had fallen hopelessly and irrevocably in love, only he'd been stupid enough to let it sift through his fingers.

He drove by every one of Lani's jobs. Nothing. Eventually he made his way back home, only to be confronted with the frantic, last-minute preparations for his fake engagement party.

Faced with only a few hours until guests were due to arrive, dinner in various stages of preparation and the house more like a home than he could ever remember it being, Colin came to a decision.

He stood in his foyer and stared down at a plant on the floor. It had a blue ribbon around it and several white flowers blooming. He had no idea what kind of plant it was, but it looked very at home.

Just another visual reminder of Lani. Somehow it strengthened his resolve. "I'm not going to give up," he told the plant. "I love her and, dammit, she's going to hear it."

"Well, it's about time."

Grimacing, he turned to face an unusually quiet Bessie and Lola.

"Fix this," Bessie demanded of him, poking him with a finger. "Because I got to tell you, Colin West, that Lani was a definite keeper."

He managed a smile. "I know." God, how he knew. "The party—"

"We'll worry about the party, you worry about your fiancée," Lola said much more kindly than her sister, patting his arm. "Just go fix this mess, darling."

He turned to leave, but suddenly Carmen was there blocking his way. She'd been hired for the day to help prepare for the party, and though she didn't look friendly, at least she hadn't stuck her tongue out at him.

Her eyes told him she thought he was one stupid man for letting Lani go. They also told him something else, and hope surged within Colin for the first time in hours.

"You know where she is," he said, trying unsuccessfully to rein in his excitement. "Tell me."

She gave him a sardonic gaze.

Damn, she couldn't talk. "I have to know, Carmen." She peered deeply into his eyes for so long he nearly yelled in frustration.

The more agitated he got, the calmer she appeared. She pointed to her ring finger, then looked at him with her eyebrows raised.

"I'll buy her a ring," he promised, but she rolled her eyes, disgusted.

What then? He would have gone running for paper and pen, but she grabbed his hand and pointed to his ring finger.

"Yes," he said urgently. "I promise, I want to marry Lani for real. I want the party tonight to be real. But I can't do any of it unless I find her. Tell me, Carmen, please, where is she?"

She searched his eyes, and he hoped to God she found what she wanted there because he had to know. Time was running out. "Tell me."

She nodded, then backed up to give herself space and started to...gyrate?

Bouncing, shimmying and shaking her bootie, she turned in a slow circle. Colin just stared at her, certain she'd cracked. "Uh...Carmen? We were talking about Lani?"

Irritated, eyes flashing, she stopped and glared at him with her hands on her hips.

"Okay, okay! Try again. I'm watching."

Again she started to writhe. No...she was hula dancing? "She's taking...dancing lessons?"

Carmen sighed loudly and shot a glance heavenward. Then she started again, definitely doing the hula for all her heavy, sixty-something-old body was worth. Colin stared at her in amazement. "She's...oh, damn. She's going to Hawaii!"

Carmen pointed to her nose and nodded triumphantly.

He was right. Lani had apparently said the hell with life and had taken off for a well-deserved vacation.

Colin hoped he could catch her or she was going to miss her own—*real*—engagement party.

13

LANI HADN'T TAKEN a vacation in...well, forever. She owed herself one, she decided.

Now seemed as good a time as any. Hawaii was calling.

In less than an hour she had a bag packed and had notified everyone that she was taking two weeks off. In another hour she was at the airport, staring at the departure screens, wondering which flight to take.

The airport was a bundle of activity around her. Voices, laughter, shouts, people rushing, walking, sleeping. Even the smells: coffee, leather, people, diesel, they all made her think of exotic places.

She was standing in front of a ticket counter before she knew it. The next flight left in minutes. If she was quick, she could be in Oahu for a late dinner. She'd lie on the beach watching the sunset, sipping pretty colored drinks.

She'd enjoy herself.

She would.

"Ma'am?" A friendly ticket agent smiled at her. "Are you next?"

She could be. With a flick of her poor, abused

credit card she could be gone. Outta here. Away from any memory of the man who'd broken her heart.

But that heart didn't want to run. It wasn't the answer, no matter how tempting, and she had to face the truth.

Yes, she'd fallen in love with a man who couldn't give that love back to her. But that wasn't a crime, nor was it his fault. He'd never misled her, not once.

Not only was she acting childishly, she'd done the one thing she'd promised she wouldn't—she'd broken her promise.

She'd let him down.

It hurt, just thinking it. How could she have done that to him?

At this very moment, Colin's mother and aunts would have staff racing madly through his house, preparing for their engagement party, the party she'd agreed to attend.

But her heart was breaking, dammit. To stand at Colin's side and pretend to love him, when she really did, would be the hardest thing in the world.

"Ma'am?"

"I'm sorry." Lani smiled apologetically. She stepped aside. "I've changed my mind."

If she lived through this heartache, she promised herself, *then* she'd travel. She'd go to Hawaii and maybe, just maybe, never come back.

But she didn't move away, not yet, just stood there

and gazed blindly at the black screen high above her, where the flight she had nearly gotten on started to blink.

They were boarding. Without her.

Then her neck was tingling, her heart racing, and slowly she turned. Standing there, chest heaving as though he'd been running, his face drawn and pale, was Colin.

"Lani."

Just her name, but he put such a wealth of feeling into it, she closed her eyes against the new onslaught of pain.

She felt his hands on her shoulders. They slid up, cupped her face, tilted it up. "Thank God, I found you in time."

Lani hadn't imagined this, what seeing him again would do to her heart.

Funny, but around them everything was normal. People rushing like ants toward their gates, hugging good-bye, laughing, smiling.

And her heart was breaking all over again.

"Please," Colin said, his voice low and raw. "Don't go. I'm so sorry I didn't understand everything sooner." His hands slid down her arms, clasped her hands tight, and in a heartrending gesture, he brought them to his lips. "Please, Lani, don't leave me."

He thought she was going.

She glanced down at her packed-to-bulging bag.

She still stood in front of the ticket counter. In one of her hands tucked in his, she held a brochure she'd picked up at the airport entrance, one that could have been mistaken for a plane ticket.

He believed she could leave him.

"I know I don't have the right to ask," he said urgently. "But if you could listen to me, just give me a few minutes, maybe I can change your mind."

She owed him. She had made a promise she had no right to break simply because of her feelings for him. She pulled her hands free and stepped back. She needed to be able to think, and she couldn't do that with his hands on her. "Colin, I'm not going—"

"I know I hurt you," he said in a rush. "I'm sorry for that, too. You're the last person in the world I wanted to hurt."

"I'm not—"

"But you threw me, Lani. You were so...real. So loyal and trusting and sweet." He came close again but didn't touch her. "So absolutely—"

"Colin, I'm not going." *It wasn't his fault*, she reminded herself. *You fell on your own, knowing he couldn't return the feelings.*

"Lani, I love you."

"I'm not— *What?*" She grabbed his shirt, hauled him closer. "What did you just say?"

"I love you."

There was a new line forming at the ticket counter behind them. It was a noisy group, but Lani managed to make herself heard. "That's a low blow, Colin," she whispered furiously. "I said I'm not going anywhere. I'll be there for your damn engagement party. You don't have to tease me by telling me—by saying— *You know!*"

He blinked at her, opened his mouth in shock, but she whirled, intending to stalk off, madder than she could ever remember being.

How dare he throw her words back in her face just so that she would come back, especially when she had already made up her mind to do so on her own.

A firm but easy hand settled at her elbow, drawing her back against the hard, warm chest she'd know anywhere. "Lani, wait."

She actually had little choice since Colin wasn't about to let her go anywhere with such a huge misunderstanding between them. Her bag fell on his foot, but he ignored the pain because it took two hands to hold her still.

The people in line seemed interested in the tussle between them but Colin didn't care.

All he cared about was keeping Lani.

Too dignified to struggle, she went limp in his arms and glared at him. "Let me go," she snapped. "I said I'm not leaving. I'll come back with you and play house, dammit, now let me go."

"You think I was toying with you," he said in disbelief, staring down into her hurting eyes. "Lani—" A frustrated growl was all he could make for a moment, he was so surprised. And hurt. "Listen to me. I've never said those words before, to anyone. *Never*, Lani. Do you understand what I'm saying to you? God, the last thing I would ever do is fling it around like a joke."

Her eyes filled, not with hope or joy, but with hurt, and he felt sick. "Am I too late?" he whispered, pulling her tight to him just to feel her body heat. "I can't be, I won't let it be too late. I love you, dammit. I'm sorry I was so slow about it, but you scared me to death."

One tear fell, but she remained silent.

Behind him, in line, several women muttered to themselves about men and their stupidity.

"No," he said fiercely, forgetting everyone that surrounded them, most of them blatantly eavesdropping now, as he hauled her closer yet, banding his arms tightly around her. "Don't cry, I'm so sorry."

"Say it again."

He pulled back slightly and stared at her.

"Say it again," she demanded.

The small crowd pressed closer, listening.

Colin's pride was gone, he had nothing left to lose. "I love you, Lani. With all my heart and soul."

But the woman in his arms didn't move a muscle, not a one, and fear filled him. Why wasn't she saying something, *anything?*

"You have to believe in me," he said, desperate

now. "I'm a slow learner but once I catch on, it's for keeps. I know now what I've been missing in my life and it's you."

Several women in the crowd let out a collective sigh.

"I know you've had it rough," he said, ignoring their audience the best he could. "I know deep down you're just as afraid as me, that you have been ever since you lost your parents so cruelly. But I can love you that much, Lani. I already do, all I need is the time to prove it to you. We can start over and make our own family."

She dipped her head down to his chest so he couldn't see her expression but he felt her shaking. God. He'd made her cry again. "I'm rushing you, I'm sorry—"

"*Rushing* me?" She lifted her head now and he saw that she hadn't been shaking with tears, but with joy. It blazed from her eyes, lighting her face and his heart.

"Colin," she said with a laugh. "I've loved you forever. You couldn't have fallen fast enough for me. *Rushing?*" She laughed again, the sound contagious.

The crowd grinned unabashedly.

"You just finally caught up with me," she said to him softly.

"Does this mean—" He didn't know, didn't have a clue and he was dying. "You're okay with... I can—"

"Promise me forever, Colin," she whispered, looping her arms around his neck.

"I'll promise you forever and a day if you promise to marry me. Fill my heart with joy and love for the rest of our lives."

She went still. "Really?"

"Marry me, Lani. For real this time."

Lani smiled, her heart overflowing. "Oh, yes," she agreed. Her future husband leaned down and kissed her, a soft, sweet, giving kiss full of love.

Above them on the departure board, the plane bound for Hawaii left the gate.

Looking For More Romance?

Visit Romance.net

Check in daily for these and other exciting features:

Hot off the press

View all current titles, and purchase them on-line.

What do the stars have in store for you?

Horoscope

Hot deals

Exclusive offers available only at Romance.net

Plus, don't miss our interactive quizzes, contests and bonus gifts.

PWEB

Back by popular demand are

DEBBIE MACOMBER's

Hard Luck, Alaska, is a
town that needs women!
And the O'Halloran brothers
are just the fellows
to fly them in.

Starting in March 2000 this beloved series returns
in special 2-in-1 collector's editions:

MAIL-ORDER MARRIAGES, featuring
Brides for Brothers and *The Marriage Risk*
On sale March 2000

FAMILY MEN, featuring
Daddy's Little Helper and *Because of the Baby*
On sale July 2000

THE LAST TWO BACHELORS, featuring
Falling for Him and *Ending in Marriage*
On sale August 2000

Collect and enjoy each MIDNIGHT SONS story!

Available at your favorite retail outlet.

HARLEQUIN®
Makes any time special ™

Temptation
BLAZE

It's hot...and it's out of control!

Pick up a **Blaze** for an experience you'll never forget. It's the bold, provocative and ultrasexy read that is sure to leave you breathless!

Join some of your favorite authors, such as Lori Foster and Vicki Lewis Thompson, for stories filled with passion and seduction.

Temptation' brings you a brand-new **Blaze** every month.

Look for it at your favorite retail outlet.

HARLEQUIN®
Makes any time special ™

Visit us at www.romance.net.

BLAZEGEN99

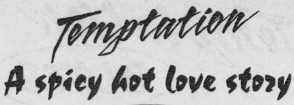

Temptation

A spicy hot love story

BLAZE

Available in February 2000

IN TOO DEEP
by
Lori Foster
(Temptation #770)

Charlotte (Charlie) Jones was used to fighting for what she wanted, and she wanted Harry Lonigan—big-time! But the sexy P.I. was doing his best to deny the steamy attraction between them. Charlie was the daughter of his best friend and father figure so, to his mind, she was off-limits. But as he worked with Charlie on an embezzling case, Charlie worked on him. Before he knew it, Harry was in too deep.

BLAZE! Red-hot reads from Temptation!

Available at your favorite retail outlet.

HARLEQUIN®
Makes any time special ™